Nova Express

Nova Express

WILLIAM S. BURROUGHS

An Evergreen Black Cat *Book*

GROVE PRESS, INC.   NEW YORK

Acknowledgment is due to Alfred A. Knopf, Inc.
for permission to quote from *The Trial* by Franz
Kafka, translated by Willa and Edwin Muir, Copy-
right © 1937, 1956, by Alfred A. Knopf, Inc.

First Evergreen Black Cat Edition 1965

Sixth Printing

MANUFACTURED IN THE UNITED STATES OF AMERICA
DISTRIBUTED BY RANDOM HOUSE, INC., NEW YORK

FOREWORD NOTE

The section called "This Horrible Case" was written in collaboration with Mr. Ian Sommerville, a mathematician—Mr. Sommerville also contributed the technical notes in the section called "Chinese Laundry"—An extension of Brion Gysin's cut-up method which I call the fold-in method has been used in this book which is consequently a composite of many writers living and dead.

Nova Express

LAST WORDS

LISTEN TO MY LAST words anywhere. Listen to my last words any world. Listen all you boards syndicates and governments of the earth. And you powers behind what filth deals consummated in what lavatory to take what is not yours. To sell the ground from unborn feet forever—

"Don't let them see us. Don't tell them what we are doing—"

Are these the words of the all-powerful boards and syndicates of the earth?

"For God's sake don't let that Coca-Cola thing out—"

"Not The Cancer Deal with The Venusians—"

"Not The Green Deal—Don't show them that—"

"Not The Orgasm Death—"

"Not the ovens—"

Listen: I call you all. Show your cards all players. Pay it all pay it all pay it *all* back. Play it all pay it all play it *all* back. For all to see. In Times Square. In Piccadilly.

"Premature. Premature. Give us a little more time."

Time for what? More lies? Premature? Premature for who? I say to all these words are not premature. These words may be too late. Minutes to go. Minutes to foe goal—

"Top Secret—Classified—For The Board—The Elite —The Initiates—"

Are these the words of the all-powerful boards and syndicates of the earth? These are the words of liars cowards collaborators traitors. Liars who want time for more lies. Cowards who can not face your "dogs" your "gooks" your "errand boys" your "human animals" with the truth. Collaborators with Insect People with Vegetable People. With any people anywhere who offer you a body forever. To shit forever. For this you have sold out your sons. Sold the ground from unborn feet forever. Traitors to all souls everywhere. You want the name of Hassan i Sabbah on your filth deeds to sell out the unborn?

What scared you all into time? Into body? Into shit? I will tell you: *the word.* Alien Word *the.* *"The"* *word* of Alien Enemy imprisons *"thee"* in Time. In Body. In Shit. Prisoner, come out. The great skies are open. I Hassan i Sabbah *rub out the word forever.* If you I cancel all your words forever. And the words of Hassan i Sabbah as also cancel. Cross all your skies see the silent writing of Brion Gysin Hassan i Sabbah: drew September 17, 1899 over New York.

Prisoners, Come Out

"Don't listen to Hassan i Sabbah," they will tell you. "He wants to take your body and all pleasures of the body away from you. Listen to us. We are serving The Garden of Delights Immortality Cosmic Consciousness The Best Ever In Drug Kicks. And *love love love* in slop buckets. How does that sound to you boys? Better than Hassan i Sabbah and his cold windy bodiless rock? Right?"

At the immediate risk of finding myself the most unpopular character of all fiction—and history is fiction— I must say this:

"Bring together state of news—Inquire onward from state to doer—Who monopolized Immortality? Who monopolized Cosmic Consciousness? Who monopolized Love Sex and Dream? Who monopolized Life Time and Fortune? Who took from you what is yours? Now they will give it all back? Did they ever give anything away for nothing? Did they ever give any more than they had to give? Did they not always take back what they gave when possible and it always was? *Listen:* Their Garden Of Delights is a terminal sewer—I have been at some pains to map this area of terminal sewage in the so called pornographic sections of *Naked Lunch* and *Soft Machine*—Their Immortality Cosmic Consciousness and Love is second-run grade-B shit—Their drugs are poison designed to beam in Orgasm Death and Nova Ovens—Stay out of the Garden Of Delights —It is a man-eating trap that ends in green goo— Throw back their ersatz Immortality—It will fall apart before you can get out of The Big Store—Flush their drug kicks down the drain—*They are poisoning and monopolizing the hallucinogen drugs—learn to make it without any chemical corn*—All that they offer is a screen to cover retreat from the colony they have so disgracefully mismanaged. To cover travel arrangements so they will never have to pay the constituents they have betrayed and sold out. Once these arrangements are complete they will blow the place up behind them.

"And what does my program of total austerity and total resistance offer *you?* I offer you nothing. I am not a politician. These are conditions of total emergency. And these are my instructions for total emergency if carried out *now* could avert the total disaster *now* on tracks:

"*Peoples of the earth, you have all been poisoned*. Convert all available stocks of morphine to apomorphine. Chemists, work round the clock on variation and synthesis of the apomorphine formulae. Apomorphine is the only agent that can disintoxicate you and cut the enemy beam off your line. Apomorphine and silence. I order total resistance directed against this conspiracy to pay off peoples of the earth in ersatz bullshit. I order total resistance directed against The Nova Conspiracy and all those engaged in it.

"The purpose of my writing is to expose and arrest Nova Criminals. In *Naked Lunch, Soft Machine* and *Nova Express* I show who they are and what they are doing and what they will do if they are not arrested. Minutes to go. Souls rotten from their orgasm drugs, flesh shuddering from their nova ovens, prisoners of the earth to *come out*. With your help we can occupy The Reality Studio and retake their universe of Fear Death and Monopoly—

"(Signed) INSPECTOR J. LEE, NOVA POLICE"

Post Script Of The Regulator: I would like to sound a word of warning—To speak is to lie—To live is to collaborate—Anybody is a coward when faced by the nova ovens—There are degrees of lying collaboration and cowardice—That is to say degrees of intoxication—It is precisely a question of *regulation*—The enemy is not man is not woman—The enemy exists only where no life is and moves always to push life into extreme untenable positions—You can cut the enemy off your line by the judicious use of apomorphine and silence—*Use the sanity drug apomorphine.*

"Apomorphine is made from morphine but its physiological action is quite different. Morphine depresses the

WILLIAM S. BURROUGHS

front brain. Apomorphine stimulates the back brain, acts on the hypothalamus to regulate the percentage of various constitutents in the blood serum and so normalize the constitution of the blood." I quote from *Anxiety and Its Treatment* by Doctor John Yerbury Dent.

Pry Yourself Loose and Listen

I was traveling with The Intolerable Kid on The Nova Lark—We were on the nod after a rumble in The Crab Galaxy involving this two-way time stock; when you come to the end of a biologic film just run it back and start over —Nobody knows the difference—Like nobody there before the film.* So they start to run it back and the projector blew up and we lammed out of there on the blast —Holed up in those cool blue mountains the liquid air in our spines listening to a little high-fi junk note fixes you right to metal and you nod out a thousand years.† Just

---

* Postulate a biologic film running from the beginning to the end, from zero to zero as all biologic film run in any time universe—Call this film X1 and postulate further that there can only be one film with the quality X1 in any given time universe. X1 is the film and performers—X2 is the audience who are all trying to get into the film—Nobody is permitted to leave the biologic theater which in this case is the human body—Because if anybody did leave the theater he would be looking at a different film Y and Film X1 and audience X2 would then cease to exist by mathematical definition—In 1960 with the publication of *Minutes To Go,* Martin's stale movie was greeted by an unprecedented chorus of boos and a concerted walkout—"We seen this five times already and not standing still for another twilight of your tired Gods."

† Since junk *is* image the effects of junk can easily be produced and concentrated in a sound and image track—Like this: Take a sick junky—Throw blue light on his so-called

sitting there in a slate house wrapped in orange flesh robes, the blue mist drifting around us when we get the call— And as soon as I set foot on Podunk earth I can smell it that burnt metal reek of nova.

"Already set off the charge," I said to I&I (Immovable and Irresistible)—"This is a burning planet—Any minute now the whole fucking shit house goes up."

So Intolerable I&I sniffs and says: "Yeah, when it happens it happens fast—This is a rush job."

And you could feel it there under your feet the whole structure buckling like a bulkhead about to blow—So the paper has a car there for us and we are driving in from the airport The Kid at the wheel and his foot on the floor— Nearly ran down a covey of pedestrians and they yell after us: "What you want to do, kill somebody?"

face or dye it blue or dye the junk blue it don't make no difference and now give him a shot and photograph the blue miracle as life pours back into that walking corpse—That will give you the image track of junk—Now project the blue change onto your own face if you want The Big Fix. The sound track is even easier—I quote from *Newsweek*, March 4, 1963 Science section: "Every substance has a characteristic set of resonant frequencies at which it vibrates or oscillates."—So you record the frequency of junk as it hits the junk-sick brain cells—

"What's that?—Brain waves are 32 or under and can't be heard? Well speed them up, God damn it—And instead of one junky concentrate me a thousand—Let there be Lexington and call a nice Jew in to run it—"

Doctor Wilhelm Reich has isolated and concentrated a unit that he calls "the orgone"—Orgones, according to W. Reich, are the units of life—They have been photographed and the color is blue—So junk sops up the orgones and that's why they need all these young junkies—They have more orgones and give higher yield of the blue concentrate on which Martin and his boys can nod out a thousand years—Martin is stealing *your orgones.*—You going to stand still for this shit?

And The Kid sticks his head out and says: "It would be a pleasure Niggers! Gooks! Terrestrial dogs"—His eyes lit up like a blow torch and I can see he is really in form—So we start right to work making our headquarters in The Land Of The Free where the call came from and which is really free and wide open for any life form the uglier the better—Well they don't come any uglier than The Intolerable Kid and your reporter—When a planet is all primed to go up they call in I&I to jump around from one faction to the other agitating and insulting all the parties before and after the fact until they all say: "By God before I give an inch the whole fucking shit house goes up in chunks."

Where we came in—You have to move fast on this job—And I&I is fast—Pops in and out of a hundred faces in a split second spitting his intolerable insults— We had the plan, what they call The Board Books to show us what is what on this dead whistle stop: Three life forms uneasily parasitic on a fourth form that is beginning to wise up. And the whole planet absolutely flapping hysterical with panic. The way we like to see them.

"This is a dead easy pitch," The Kid says.

"Yeah," I say. "A little bit too easy. Something here, Kid. Something wrong. I can feel it."

But The Kid can't hear me. Now all these life forms came from the most intolerable conditions: hot places, cold places, terminal stasis and the last thing any of them want to do is go back where they came from. And The Intolerable Kid is giving out with such pleasantries like this:

"All right take your ovens out with you and pay Hitler on the way out. Nearly got the place hot enough for you Jews didn't he?"

"Know about Niggers? Why darkies were born? Antennae coolers what else? Always a spot for *good* Darkies."

17

"You cunts constitute a disposal problem in the worst form there is and raise the nastiest whine ever heard anywhere: 'Do you love me? Do you love me? Do you love me???' Why don't you go back to Venus and fertilize a forest?"

"And as for you White Man Boss, you dead prop in Martin's stale movie, you terminal time junky, haul your heavy metal ass back to Uranus. Last shot at the door. You need one for the road." By this time everybody was even madder than they were shit scared. But I&I figured things were moving too slow.

"We need a peg to hang it on," he said. "Something really ugly like virus. Not for nothing do they come from a land without mirrors." So he takes over this newsmagazine.

"Now," he said, "I'll by God show them how ugly the Ugly American can be."

And he breaks out all the ugliest pictures in the image bank and puts it out on the subliminal so one crisis piles up after the other right on schedule. And I&I is whizzing around like a buzz saw and that black nova laugh of his you can hear it now down all the streets shaking the buildings and skyline like a stage prop. But me I am looking around and the more I look the less I like what I see. For one thing the nova heat is moving in fast and heavy like I never see it anywhere else. But I&I just says I have the copper jitters and turns back to his view screen: "They are skinning the chief of police alive in some jerkwater place. Want to sit in?"

"Naw," I said. "Only interested in my own skin."

And I walk out thinking who I *would* like to see skinned alive. So I cut into the Automat and put coins into the fish cake slot and then I really see it: Chinese partisans and well armed with vibrating static and image guns. So I throw down the fish cakes with tomato sauce and make it back to the office where The Kid is still glued to that screen. He looks up smiling dirty and says:

"Wanta molest a child and disembowel it right after?"

"Pry yourself loose and listen." And I tell him. "Those Tiddly Winks don't fuck around you know."

"So what?" he says. "I've still got The Board Books. I can split this whistle stop wide open tomorrow."

No use talking to him. I look around some more and find out the blockade on planet earth is broken. Explorers moving in whole armies. And everybody concerned is fed up with Intolerable I&I. And all he can say is: "So what? I've still got . . . /" Cut.

"Board Books taken. The film reeks of burning switch like a blow torch. Prerecorded heat glare massing Hiroshima. This whistle stop wide open to hot crab people. Mediation? Listen: Your army is getting double zero in floor by floor game of 'symbiosis.' Mobilized reasons to love Hiroshima and Nagasaki? Virus to maintain terminal sewers of Venus?"

"All nations sold out by liars and cowards. Liars who want time for the future negatives to develop stall you with more lying offers while hot crab people mass war to extermination with the film in Rome. These reports reek of nova, sold out job, shit birth and death. Your planet has been invaded. You are dogs on all tape. The entire planet is being developed into terminal identity and complete surrender."

"But suppose film death in Rome doesn't work and we can get every male body even madder than they are shit scared? We need a peg to evil full length. By God show them how ugly the ugliest pictures in the dark room can be. Pitch in the oven ambush. Spill all the board gimmicks. This symbiosis con? Can tell you for sure 'symbiosis' is ambush straight to the ovens. 'Human dogs' to be eaten alive under white hot skies of Minraud."

And Intolerable I&I's "errand boys" and "strikebreakers" are copping out right left and center:

"Mr. Martin, and you board members, vulgar stupid Americans, you will regret calling in the Mayan Aztec

Gods with your synthetic mushrooms. Remember we keep exact junk measure of the pain inflicted and that pain must be paid in full. Is that clear enough Mr. Intolerable Martin, or shall I make it even clearer? Allow me to introduce myself: The Mayan God of Pain And Fear from the white hot plains of Venus which does not mean a God of vulgarity, cowardice, ugliness and stupidity. There is a cool spot on the surface of Venus three hundred degrees cooler than the surrounding area. I have held that spot against all contestants for five hundred thousand years. Now you expect to use me as your 'errand boy' and 'strikebreaker' summoned up by an IBM machine and a handful of virus crystals? How long could you hold that spot, you 'board members'? About thirty seconds I think with all your guard dogs. And you thought to channel my energies for 'operation total disposal'? Your 'operations' there or here this or that come and go and are no more. *Give my name back.* That name must be paid for. You have not paid. My name is not yours to use. Henceforth I think about thirty seconds is written."

And you can see the marks are wising up, standing around in sullen groups and that mutter gets louder and louder. Any minute now fifty million adolescent gooks will hit the street with switch blades, bicycle chains and cobblestones.

"Street gangs, Uranian born of nova conditions, get out and fight for your streets. Call in the Chinese and any random factors. Cut all tape. Shift cut tangle magpie voice lines of the earth. Know about The Board's 'Green Deal?' They plan to board the first life boat in drag and leave 'their human dogs' under the white hot skies of Venus. 'Operation Sky Switch' also known as 'Operation Total Disposal.' All right you board bastards, we'll by God show you 'Operation Total Exposure.' For all to see. In Times Square. In Piccadilly."

SO PACK YOUR ERMINES

"SO PACK YOUR ERMINES, Mary—We are getting out of here right now—I've seen this happen before—The marks are coming up on us—And the heat is moving in—Recollect when I was traveling with Limestone John on The Carbonic Caper—It worked like this: He rents an amphitheater with marble walls he is a stone painter you dig can create a frieze while you wait—So he puts on a diving suit like the old Surrealist Lark and I am up on a high pedestal pumping the air to him—Well, he starts painting on the limestone walls with hydrochloric acid and jetting himself around with air blasts he can cover the wall in ten seconds, carbon dioxide settling down on the marks begin to cough and loosen their collars."

"But what is he painting?"

"Why it's arrg a theater full of people suffocating—"

So we turn the flops over and move on—If you keep it practical they can't hang a nova rap on you—Well, we hit this town and right away I don't like it.

"Something here, John—Something wrong—I can feel it—"

But he says I just have the copper jitters since the

nova heat moved in—Besides we are cool, just rolling flops is all three thousand years in show business—So he sets up his amphitheater in a quarry and begins lining up the women clubs and poets and window dressers and organizes this "Culture Fest" he calls it and I am up in the cabin of a crane pumping the air to him— Well the marks are packing in, the old dolls covered with ice and sapphires and emeralds are really magnificent—So I think maybe I was wrong and everything is cool when I see like fifty young punks have showed in aqualungs carrying fish spears and without thinking I yell out from the crane:

"Izzy The Push—Sammy The Butcher—*Hey Rube!*"

Meanwhile I have forgotten the air pump and The Carbonic Kid is turning blue and trying to say something—I rush and pump some air to him and he yells:

"No! No! No!"

I see other marks are coming on with static and camera guns, Sammy and the boys are not making it— These kids have pulled the reverse switch—At this point The Blue Dinosaur himself charged out to discover what the beef is and starts throwing his magnetic spirals at the rubes—They just moved back ahead of him until he runs out of charge and stops. Next thing the nova heat slipped antibiotic handcuffs on all of us.

Naborhood in Aqualungs

I was traveling with Merit John on The Carbonic Caper—Larceny with a crew of shoppers—And this number comes over the air to him—So he starts painting The D Fence last Spring—And shitting himself around with air blasts in Hicksville—Stopped ten seconds and our carbon dioxide gave out and we began to cough for such a purpose suffocating under a potted palm in the lobby—

"Move on, you dig, copping out 'The Fish Poison Con.' "

"I got you—Keep it practical and they can't—"

Transported back to South America we hit this town and right away being stung by the dreaded John—He never missed—Burned three thousand years in me playing cop and quarry—So the marks are packing in virus and subject to dissolve and everything is cool—Assimilate ice sapphires and emeralds all regular—So I walk in about fifty young punks—Sammy and the boys are all he had —One fix—Pulled the reverse switch—Traveling store closing so I don't work like this—John set my medications—Nagasaki in acid on the walls faded out under the rubber trees—He can cover feet back to 1910—We could buy it settling down—Lay up in the Chink laundry on the collars—

"But what stale rooming house flesh—"

Cradles old troupers—Like Cleopatra applying the asp hang a Nova Rap on you—

"Lush?—I don't like it—Empty pockets in the worn metal—Feel it?"

But John says: "Copper jitters since the space sell— The old doll is covered—"

Heavy and calm holding cool leather armchair—Organizes this wispy mustache—I stopped in front of a mirror—Really magnificent in a starched collar—It is a naborhood in aqualungs with free lunch everywhere yell out "Sweet Sixteen"—I walked without Izzy The Push—

"Hey Rube!!"

Came to the Chinese laundry meanwhile—I have forgotten the Chink in front—Fix words hatch The Blue Dinosaur—I was reading them back magnetic—Only way to orient yourself—Traveling with the Chink kid John set throat like already written—"Stone Reading" we call it in the trade—While you wait he packs in Rome—I've checked the diving suit like every night—Up on a high pedestal perform this unnatural act—In acid on the walls —Set your watch by it—So that gives us twenty marks out through the side window and collars—

"But what in St. Louis?"

Memory picture coming in—So we turn over silver sets and banks and clubs as old troupers—Nova Rap on you that night as we walked out—I don't like it—Something picking up laundry and my flesh feel it—

But John says: "Afternoon copper jitters since the caper—Housebreaking can cause this—"

We are cool just rolling—when things go wrong once —show business—We can't find poets and organize this cut and the flesh won't work—And there we are with the air off like bleached idiots—Well I think maybe kicks from our condition—They took us—The old dolls on a train burning junk—Thawing flesh showed in aqualungs— Steam a yell out from the crane—

"Hey Rube!!"

Three silver digits explode—Meanwhile I have forgotten streets of Madrid—And clear as sunlight pump some air to him and he said: "Que tal Henrique?"

I am standing through an invisible door click the air to him—Well we hit this town and right away aphrodisiac ointment—

"Doc goofed here, John—Something wrong—Too much Spanish."

"What? It's green see? A green theater—"

So we turn the marks over and rent a house as old troupers—And we flush out this cool pure Chinese H from show business—And he starts the whole Green Rite and organizes this fibrous grey amphitheater in old turnip—Meanwhile I have forgotten a heavy blue silence —Carbonic Kid is turning to cold liquid metal and run pump some air to him in a blue mist of vaporized flicker helmets—The metal junkies were not making it—These kids intersected The Nova Police—We are just dust falls from demagnetized patterns—Show business—Calendar in Weimar youths—Faded poets in the silent amphitheater —His block house went away through this air—Click St. Louis under drifting soot—And I think maybe I was in old clinic—Outside East St. Louis—Really magnificent for two notes a week—Meanwhile I had forgotten "Mother"—Wouldn't you?—Doc Benway and The Carbonic Kid turning a rumble in Dallas involving this pump goofed on ether and mixed in flicker helmets—

"He is gone through this town and right away tape recorders of his voice behind, John—Something wrong —I can pose a colorless question??"

"Is all right—I just have the silence—Word dust falls three thousand years through an old blue calendar—"

"William, no me hagas caso—People who told me I could move on you copping out—said 'Good-Bye' to William and 'Keep it practical' and I could hear him hit this town and right away I closed the door when I saw John—Something wrong—Invisible hotel room is all— I just have the knife and he said:

"Nova Heat moved in at the seams—Like three thousand years in hot claws at the window'—

"And Meester William in Tétuan and said: 'I have gimmick is cool and all very technical—These colorless sheets are the air pump and I can see the flesh when it has color—Writing say some message that is coming on all flesh—'

"And I said: 'William tu es loco—Pulled the reverse switch—No me hagas while you wait'—Kitchen knife in the heart—Feel it—Gone away—Pulled the reverse switch —Place no good—No bueno—He pack caso—William tu hagas yesterday call—These colorless sheets are empty —You can look any place—No good—No bueno—Adios Meester William—"

The Fish Poison Con

I was traveling with Merit Inc. checking store attendants for larceny with a crew of "shoppers"—There was two middle-aged cunts one owning this chihuahua which whimpered and yapped in a cocoon of black sweaters and Bob Schafer Crew Leader who was an American Fascist with Roosevelt jokes—It happens in Iowa this number comes over the car radio: "Old Sow Got Caught In The Fence Last Spring"—And Schafer said "Oh my God, are we ever in Hicksville." Stopped that night in Pleasantville Iowa and our tires gave out we had no tire rations during the war for such a purpose —And Bob got drunk and showed his badge to the locals in a road house by the river—And I ran into The Sailor under a potted palm in the lobby—We hit the local croakers with "the fish poison con"—"I got these poison fish, Doc, in the tank transported back from South America I'm a Ichthyologist and after being stung by the dreaded Candirú—Like fire through the blood is it not? Doctor, and coming on now"—And The Sailor goes into his White Hot Agony Act chasing the doctor around his office like a blowtorch He never missed—But he burned down the croakers—So like Bob and me when we "had a catch" as the old cunts call it and arrested some sulky clerk with his hand deep in the company pocket, we take turns playing the tough cop and the con cop—So I walk in on this Pleasantville croaker and tell him I have contracted this Venusian virus and subject to dissolve myself in poison juices and assimilate the passers-by unless I get my medicine and get it regular—So I walk in on this old party smelling like a compost heap and steaming demurely and he snaps at me, "What's *your* trouble?"

"The Venusian Gook Rot, doctor."

"Now see here young man my time is valuable."

"Doctor, this is a medical emergency."

Old shit but good—I walked out on the nod—

"All he had was one fix, Sailor."

"You're loaded—You assimilated the croaker—Left me sick—"

"Yes. He was old and tough but not too tough for The Caustic Enzymes Of Woo."

The Sailor was thin and the drugstore was closing so I didn't want him to get physical and disturb my medications—The next croaker wrote with erogenous acid vats on one side and Nagasaki Ovens on the other —And we nodded out under the rubber trees with the long red carpet under our feet back to 1910—We could buy it in the drugstore tomorrow—Or lay up in the Chink laundry on the black smoke—drifting through stale rooming houses, pool halls and chili—Fell back on sad flesh small and pretentious in a theatrical boarding house the aging ham cradles his tie up and stabs a vein like Cleopatra applying the asp—Click back through the cool grey short-change artists—lush rolling ghosts of drunken sleep—Empty pockets in the worn metal subway dawn—

I woke up in the hotel lobby the smell heavy and calm holding a different body molded to the leather chair —I was sick but not needle sick—This was a black smoke yen—The Sailor still sleeping and he looked very young under a wispy mustache—I woke him up and he looked around with slow hydraulic control his eyes unbluffed unreadable—

"Let's make the street—I'm thin—"

I was in fact very thin I saw when I stopped in front of a mirror panel and adjusted my tie knot in a starched collar—It was a naborhood of chili houses and cheap saloons with free lunch everywhere and heavy calm bartenders humming "Sweet Sixteen"—I walked without thinking like a horse will and came to The Chinese Laundry by Clara's Massage Parlor—We siphoned in and The Chink in front jerked one eye back and went on ironing a shirt front—We walked through a door and a curtain and the black smoke set our lungs dancing The Junky Jig and we lay up on our junk hip while a Chinese kid cooked our pills and handed us the pipe—After six pipes we smoke slow and order a pot of tea the Chink kid goes out fix it and the words hatch in my throat like already written there I was reading them back—"Lip Reading" we call it in the trade only way to orient yourself when in Rome—"I've checked the harness bull—He comes in McSorley's every night at 2:20 A.M. and forces the local pederast to perform this unnatural act on his person—So regular you can set your watch by it: 'I won't—I won't—Not again—Glub—Glub—Glub.' "—"So that gives us twenty minutes at least to get in and out through the side window and eight hours start we should be in St. Louis before they miss the time—Stop off and see The Family"—Memory pictures coming in—Little Boy Blue and all the heavy silver sets and banks and clubs—Cool heavy eyes moving steel and oil shares —I had a rich St. Louis family—It was set for that night—As we walked out I caught the Japanese girl picking up laundry and my flesh crawled under the junk and I made a meet for her with the afternoon— Good plan to make sex before a caper—Housebreaking can cause this wet dream sex tension especially when things go wrong—(Once in Peoria me and The Sailor charged a drugstore and we can't find the jimmy for the narco cabinet and the flash won't work and the harness bull sniffing round the door and there we are with The Sex Current giggling ourselves off like beached idiots—Well the cops got such nasty kicks from our condition they took us to the RR station and we get on a train shivering burning junk sick and the warm vegetable smells of thawing flesh and stale come slowly filled the car—Nobody could look at us steaming away there like manure piles—) I woke out of a light yen sleep when the Japanese girl came in—Three silver digits exploded in my head—I walked out into streets of Madrid and won a football pool—Felt the Latin mind clear and banal as sunlight met Paco by the soccer scores and he said: "Que tal Henrique?"

And I went to see my amigo who was taking medicina again and he had no money to give me and didn't want to do anything but take more medicina and stood there waiting for me to leave so he could take it after saying he was not going to take any more so I said, "William no me hagas caso." And met a Cuban that night in The Mar Chica who told me I could work in his band—The next day I said good-bye to William and there was nobody there to listen and I could hear him reaching for his medicina and needles as I closed the door—When I saw the knife I knew Meester William was death disguised as any other person—Pues I saw El Hombre Invisible in a hotel room somewhere tried to reach him with the knife and he said: "If you kill me this crate will come apart at the seams like a rotten undervest"—And I saw a monster crab with hot claws at the window and Meester William took some white medicina and vomited into the toilet and we escaped to Greece with a boy about my age who kept calling Meester William "The Stupid American"—And Meester William looked like a hypnotist I saw once in Tétuan and said: "I have gimmick to beat The Crab but it is very technical"—And we couldn't read what he was writing on transparent sheets—In Paris he showed me

The Man who paints on these sheets pictures in the air
—And The Invisible Man said:

"These colorless sheets are what flesh is made from—
Becomes flesh when it has color and writing—That is
Word And Image write the message that is you on
colorless sheets determine all flesh."

And I said: "William, tu éres loco."

No Good—No Bueno

So many years—that image—got up and fixed in the
sick dawn—*No me hagas caso*—Again he touched like
that—smell of dust—The tears gathered—In Mexico
again he touched—Codeine pills powdered out into the
cold Spring air—Cigarette holes in the vast Thing
Police—Could give no information other than wind
identity fading out—dwindling—"Mr. Martin" couldn't
reach is all—Bread knife in the heart—Shadow turned
off the lights and water—We intersect on empty walls
—Look anywhere—No good—Falling in the dark mutinous door—Dead Hand stretching zero—Five times
of dust we made it all the living and the dead—Young
form went to Madrid—Demerol by candlelight—Wind
hand—The Last Electrician to tap on pane—Migrants
arrival—Poison of dead sun went away and sent papers
—Ferry boat cross flutes of Ramadan—Dead muttering in the dog's space—Cigarette hole in the dark—
give no information other than the cold Spring cemetery—The Sailor went wrong in corridors of that hospital—Thing Police keep all Board Room Reports is
all—Bread knife in the heart proffers the disaster accounts
—He just sit down on "Mr. Martin"—Couldn't reach
flesh on Niño Perdido—A long time between flutes of
Ramadan—No me hagas caso sliding between light and
shadow—

WILLIAM S. BURROUGHS

"The American trailing cross the wounded galaxies con su medicina, William."

Half your brain slowly fading—Turned off the lights and water—Couldn't reach flesh—empty walls—Look anywhere—Dead on tracks see Mr. Bradly Mr. Zero—And being blind may not refuse the maps to my blood whom I created—"Mr. Bradly Mr. Martin," couldn't you write us any better than that?—Gone away—You can look any place—No good—No bueno—

I spit blood under the sliding vulture shadows—At The Mercado Mayorista saw a tourist—A Meester Merican fruto drinking pisco—and fixed me with the eyes so I sit down and drink and tell him how I live in a shack under the hill with a tin roof held down by rocks and hate my brothers because they eat—He says something about "malo viento" and laughs and I went with him to a hotel I know—In the morning he says I am honest and will I come with him to Pucallpa he is going into the jungle looking for snakes and spiders to take pictures and bring them back to Washington they always carry something away even if it is only a spider monkey spitting blood the way most of us do here in the winter when the mist comes down from the mountains and never leaves your clothes and lungs and everyone coughed and spit blood mist on the mud floor where I sleep—We start out next day in a Mixto Bus by night we are in the mountains with snow and the Meester brings out a bottle of pisco and the driver gets drunk down into the Selva came to Pucallpa three days later—The Meester locates a brujo and pays him to prepare Ayuhuasca and I take some too and muy mareado—Then I was back in Lima and other places I didn't know and saw the Meester as child in a room with rose wallpaper looking at something I couldn't see—Tasting roast beef and turkey and ice cream in my throat knowing the thing I couldn't see was always

31

out there in the hall—And the Meester was looking at me and I could see the street boy words there in his throat—Next day the police came looking for us at the hotel and the Meester showed letters to the Commandante so they shook hands and went off to lunch and I took a bus back to Lima with money he gave me to buy equipment—

Shift Coordinate Points

K9 was in combat with the alien mind screen—Magnetic claws feeling for virus punch cards—pulling him into vertiginous spins—

"Back—Stay out of those claws—Shift coordinate points—" By Town Hall Square long stop for the red light—A boy stood in front of the hot dog stand and blew water from his face—Pieces of grey vapor drifted back across wine gas and brown hair as hotel faded photo showed a brass bed—Unknown mornings blew rain in cobwebs—Summer evenings feel to a room with rose wallpaper—Sick dawn whisper of clock hands and brown hair—Morning blew rain on copper roofs in a slow haze of apples—Summer light on rose wallpaper—Iron mesas lit by a pink volcano—Snow slopes under the Northern shirt—Unknown street stirring sick dawn whispers of junk—Flutes of Ramadan in the distance—St. Louis lights wet cobblestones of future life—Fell through the urinal and the bicycle races—On the bar wall the clock hands—My death across his face faded through the soccer scores—smell of dust on the surplus army blankets—Stiff jeans against one wall—And KiKi went away like a cat—Some clean shirt and walked out—He is gone through unknown morning blew—"No good—No bueno—Hustling myself—" Such wisdom in gusts—

K9 moved back into the combat area—Standing now

in the Chinese youth sent the resistance message jolting clicking tilting through the pinball machine—Enemy plans exploded in a burst of rapid calculations—Clicking in punch cards of redirected orders—Crackling shortwave static—Bleeeeeeeeeeeeeeep—Sound of thinking metal—

"Calling partisans of all nations—Word falling—Photo falling—Break through in Grey Room—Pinball led streets —Free doorways—Shift coordinate points—"

"The ticket that exploded posed little time so I'll say 'good night'—Pieces of grey Spanish Flu wouldn't photo —Light the wind in green neon—You at the dog—The street blew rain—If you wanted a cup of tea with rose wallpaper—The dog turns—So many and sooo—"

"In progress I am mapping a photo—Light verse of wounded galaxies at the dog I did—The street blew rain—The dog turns—Warring head intersected Powers —Word falling—Photo falling—Break through in Grey Room—"

He is gone away through invisible mornings leaving a million tape recorders of his voice behind fading into the cold spring air pose a colorless question?

"The silence fell heavy and blue in mountain villages—Pulsing mineral silence as word dust falls from demagnetized patterns—Walked through an old blue calendar in Weimar youth—Faded photo on rose wallpaper under a copper roof—In the silent dawn little grey men played in his block house and went away through an invisible door—Click St. Louis under drifting soot of old newspapers—'Daddy Longlegs' looked like Uncle Sam on stilts and he ran this osteopath clinic outside East St. Louis and took in a few junky patients for two notes a week they could stay on the nod in green lawn chairs and look at the oaks and grass stretching down to a little lake in the sun and the nurse moved around the lawn with her silver trays feeding the junk in—We called her 'Mother'—Wouldn't you?—Doc Benway and me was holed up there after a rumble in Dallas involving this aphrodisiac ointment and Doc goofed on ether and mixed in too much Spanish Fly and burned the prick right off the Police Commissioner straight away—So we come to 'Daddy Longlegs' to cool off and found him cool and casual in a dark room with potted rubber plants and a silver tray on the table where he liked to see a week in advance—The nurse showed us to a room with rose wallpaper and we had this bell any hour of the day or night ring and the nurse charged in with a loaded hypo—Well one day we were sitting out in the lawn chairs with lap robes it was a fall day trees turning and the sun cold on the lake—Doc picks up a piece of grass—

"Junk turns you on vegetable—It's green, see?—A green fix should last a long time."

We checked out of the clinic and rented a house and Doc starts cooking up this green junk and the basement was full of tanks smelled like a compost heap of junkies —So finally he draws off this heavy green fluid and loads it into a hypo big as a bicycle pump—

"Now we must find a worthy vessel," he said and we flush out this old goof ball artist and told him it was pure Chinese H from The Ling Dynasty and Doc shoots the whole pint of green right into the main line and the Yellow Jacket turns fibrous grey green and withered up like an old turnip and I said: "I'm getting out of here, me," and Doc said: "An unworthy vessel obviously—So I have now decided that junk is not green but blue."

So he buys a lot of tubes and globes and they are flickering in the basement this battery of tubes metal vapor and quicksilver and pulsing blue spheres and a smell of ozone and a little high-fi blue note fixed you right to metal this junk note tinkling through your crystals and a heavy blue silence fell *klunk*—and all the words turned to cold liquid metal and ran off you man just fixed there in a cool blue mist of vaporized bank notes—We found out later that the metal junkies were all radioactive and subject to explode if two of them came into contact—At this point in our researches we intersected The Nova Police—

CHINESE LAUNDRY

Chinese Laundry

WHEN YOUNG SUTHERLAND asked me to procure him a commission with the nova police, I jokingly answered: "Bring in Winkhorst, technician and chemist for The Lazarus Pharmaceutical Company, and we will discuss the matter."

"Is this Winkhorst a nova criminal?"

"No just a technical sergeant wanted for interrogation."

I was thinking of course that he knew nothing of the methods by which such people are brought in for interrogation—It is a precision operation—First we send out a series of agents—(usually in the guise of journalists)—to contact Winkhorst and expose him to a battery of stimulus units—The contact agents talk and record the response on all levels to the word units while a photographer takes pictures—This material is passed along to The Art Department—Writers write "Winkhorst," painters paint "Winkhorst," a method actor *becomes*

"Winkhorst," and then "Winkhorst" will answer our questions—The processing of Winkhorst was already under way—

Some days later there was a knock at my door—Young Sutherland was standing there and next to him a man with coat collar turned up so only the eyes were visible spitting indignant protest—I noticed that the overcoat sleeves were empty.

"I have him in a strait jacket," said Sutherland propelling the man into my room—"This is Winkhorst."

I saw that the collar was turned up to conceal a gag—"But—You misunderstood me—Not on this level—I mean really—"

"You said bring in Winkhorst didn't you?"

I was thinking fast: "All right—Take off the gag and the strait jacket."

"But he'll scream the fuzz in—"

"No he won't."

As he removed the strait jacket I was reminded of an old dream picture—This process is known as retroactive dreaming—Performed with precision and authority becomes accomplished fact—If Winkhorst did start screaming no one would hear him—Far side of the world's mirror moving into my past—Wall of glass you know—Winkhorst made no attempt to scream—Iron cool he sat down—I asked Sutherland to leave us promising to put his application through channels—

"I have come to ask settlement for a laundry bill," Winkhorst said.

"What laundry do you represent?"

"The Chinese laundry."

"The bill will be paid through channels—As you know nothing is more complicated and time consuming than processing requisition orders for so-called 'personal expenses'—And you know also that it is strictly forbidden to offer currency in settlement."

"I was empowered to ask a settlement—Beyond that I know nothing—And now may I ask why I have been summoned?"

"Let's not say summoned—Let us just say invited—It's more humane that way you see—Actually we are taking an opinion poll in regard to someone with whom I believe you have a long and close association, namely Mr. Winkhorst of The Lazarus Pharmaceutical Company—We are interviewing friends, relatives, coworkers to predict his chances for reelection as captain of the chemical executive softball team—You must of course realize the importance of this matter in view of the company motto 'Always play *soft* ball' is it not?—Now just to give the interview life let us pretend that you are yourself Winkhorst and I will put the questions directly ketch?—Very well Mr. Winkhorst, let's not waste time—We know that you are the chemist responsible for synthesizing the new hallucinogen drugs many of which have not yet been released even for experimental purposes —We know also that you have effected certain molecular alterations in the known hallucinogens that are being freely distributed in many quarters—Precisely how are these alterations effected?—Please do not be deterred from making a complete statement by my obvious lack of technical knowledge—That is not my job—Your answers will be recorded and turned over to the Technical Department for processing."

"The process is known as stress deformation—It is done or was done with a cyclotron—For example the mescaline molecule is exposed to cyclotron stress so that the energy field is deformed and some molecules are activated on fissionable level—Mescaline so processed will be liable to produce, in the human subject—(known as 'canine preparations')—uh unpleasant and dangerous symptoms and in particular 'the heat syndrome' which is a reflection of nuclear fission—Subjects complain they are on fire, confined in a suffocating furnace, white hot bees swarming in the body—The hot bees are of course the deformed mescaline molecules —I am putting it simply of course—"

"There are other procedures?"

"Of course but always it is a question of deformation or association on a molecular level—Another procedure consists in exposing the mescaline molecule to certain virus cultures—The virus as you know is a very small particle and can be precisely associated on molecular chains—This association gives an additional tune-in with anybody who has suffered from a virus infection such as hepatitis for example—Much easier to produce the heat syndrome in such a preparation."

"Can this process be reversed? That is can you decontaminate a compound once the deformation has been effected?"

"Not so easy—It would be simpler to recall our stock from the distributors and replace it."

"And now I would like to ask you if there could be benign associations—Could you for example associate mescaline with apomorphine on a molecular level?"

"First we would have to synthesize the apomorphine formulae—As you know it is forbidden to do this."

"And for very good reason is it not, Winkhorst?"

"Yes—Apomorphine combats parasite invasion by stimulating the regulatory centers to normalize metabolism—A powerful variation of this drug could deactivate all verbal units and blanket the earth in silence, disconnecting the entire heat syndrome."

"You could do this, Mr. Winkhorst?"

"It would not be easy—certain technical details and so little time—" He held up his thumb and forefinger a quarter inch apart.

"Difficult but not impossible, Mr. Winkhorst?"

"Of course not—If I receive the order—This is unlikely in view of certain facts known to both of us."

"You refer to the scheduled nova date?"

"Of course."

"You are convinced that this is inevitable, Mr. Winkhorst?"

"I have seen the formulae—I do not believe in miracles."

"Of what do these formulae consist, Mr. Winkhorst?"

"It is a question of disposal—What is known as Uranium and this applies to all such raw material is actually a form of excrement—The disposal problem of radioactive waste in any time universe is ultimately insoluble."

"But if we disintegrate verbal units, that is vaporize the containers, then the explosion could not take place in effect would never have existed—"

"Perhaps—I am a chemist not a prophet—It is considered axiomatic that the nova formulae can not be broken, that the process is irreversible once set in motion—All energy and appropriations is now being channeled into escape plans—If you are interested I am empowered to make an offer of evacuation—on a time level of course."

"And in return?"

"You will simply send back a report that there is no evidence of nova activity on planet earth."

"What you are offering me is a precarious aqualung existence in somebody else's stale movie—Such people made a wide U turn back to the '20s—Besides the whole thing is ridiculous—Like I send back word from Mercury: 'The climate is cool and bracing—The natives are soo friendly'—or 'On Uranus one is conscious of a lightness in the limbs and an exhilarating sense of freedom' —So Doctor Benway snapped, 'You will simply send back spitting notice on your dirty nova activity—It is ridiculous like when the egg cracks the climate is cool and bracing'—or 'Uranus is mushrooming freedom'—This is the old splintered pink carnival 1917—Sad little irrigation ditch—Where else if they have date twisting paralyzed in the blue movies?—You are offering me aqualung scraps —precarious flesh—soiled movie, rag on cock—Intestinal street boy smells through the outhouse.' "

"I am empowered to make the offer not assess its validity."

"The offer is declined—The so-called officers on this planet have panicked and are rushing the first life boat in drag—Such behavior is unbecoming an officer and these people have been relieved of a command they evidently experienced as an intolerable burden in any case—In all my experience as a police officer I have never seen such a downright stupid conspiracy—The nova mob operating here are stumble bums who couldn't even crash our police line-up anywhere else—"

This is the old needling technique to lure a criminal out into the open—Three thousand years with the force and it still works—Winkhorst was fading out in hot spirals of the crab nebula—I experienced a moment of panic— walked slowly to the tape recorder—

"Now if you would be so kind, Mr. Winkhorst, I would like you to listen to this music and give me your reaction —We are using it in a commercial on the apomorphine program—Now if you would listen to this music and give me advantage—We are thinking of sullen street boy for this spot—"

I put on some Gnaova drum music and turned around both guns blazing—Silver needles under tons focus come level on average had opened up still as good as he used to be pounding stabbing to the drum beats—The scorpion controller was on screen blue eyes white hot spitting from the molten core of a planet where lead melts at noon, his body half concealed by the portico of a Mayan temple—A stink of torture chambers and burning flesh filled the room—Prisoners staked out under the white hot skies of Minraud eaten alive by metal ants—I kept distance surrounding him with pounding stabbing light blasts seventy tons to the square inch—The orders loud and clear now: "Blast—Pound—Strafe—Stab—*Kill*"—The screen opened out—I could see Mayan codices and Egyptian hieroglyphs—Prisoners screaming in the ovens broken down to insect forms—Life-sized portrait of a pantless corpse hanged to a telegraph pole ejaculating under a white hot sky—Stink of torture when the egg cracks— always to insect forms—Staked out spines gathering mushroom ants—Eyes pop out naked hanged to a telegraph pole of adolescent image—

The music shifted to Pan Pipes and I moved away to remote mountain villages where blue mist swirled through the slate houses—Place of the vine people under eternal moonlight—Pressure removed—Seventy tons to the square inch suddenly moved out—From a calm grey distance I saw the scorpion controller explode in the low pressure area—Great winds whipping across a black plain scattered the codices and hieroglyphs to rubbish heaps of the earth—(A Mexican boy whistling Mambo, drops his pants by a mud wall and wipes his ass with a page from the Madrid codex) Place of the dust people who live in sand storms riding the wind—*Wind wind wind* through dusty offices and archives—Wind through the board rooms and torture banks of time—

("A great calm shrouds the green place of the vine people.")

Inflexible Authority

When I handed in my report to The District Supervisor he read it through with a narrow smile—"They have

43

distracted you with a war film and given false information as usual—You are inexperienced of course—Totally green troops in the area—However your unauthorized action will enable us to cut some corners—Now come along and we will get the real facts—"

The police patrol pounded into the home office of Lazarus & Co—

"And now Mr. Winkhorst and you gentlemen of the board, let's have the real story and quickly or would you rather talk to the partisans?"

"You dumb hicks."

"The information and quickly—We have no time to waste with such as you."

The D.S. stood there translucent silver sending a solid blast of inflexible authority.

"All right—We'll talk—The cyclotron processes image —It's the microfilm principle—smaller and smaller, more and more images in less space pounded down under the cyclotron to crystal image meal—We can take the whole fucking planet out that way up our ass in a finger stall— Image of both of us good as he used to be—A *stall* you dig—Just old showmen packing our ermines you might say—"

"Enough of that show—Continue please with your statement."

"Sure, sure, but you see now why we had to laugh till we pissed watching those dumb rubes playing around with photomontage—Like charging a regiment of tanks with a defective slingshot."

"For the last time out of me—Continue with your statement."

"Sure, sure, but you see now why we had such look-out on these dumb rubes playing around with a splintered carnival—Charging a regiment of tanks with a defective sanitarium 1917—Never could keep his gas—Just an old trouper is all"—(He goes into a song and dance routine dancing off stage—An 1890 cop picks him up in the wings and brings back a ventriloquist dummy.)

"This, gentlemen, is a death dwarf—As you can see manipulated by remote control—Compliments of Mr. & Mrs. D."

"Give me a shot," says the dwarf. "And I'll tell you something interesting."

Hydraulic metal hands proffer a tray of phosphorescent meal yellow brown in color like pulverized amber—The dwarf takes out a hypo from a silver case and shoots a pinch of the meal in the main line.

"Images—millions of images—That's what I eat— Cyclotron shit—Ever try kicking *that* habit with apomorphine?—Now I got all the images of sex acts and torture ever took place anywhere and I can just blast it out and control you gooks right down to the molecule—I got orgasms—I got screams—I got all the images any hick poet ever shit out—My Power's coming— My Power's coming—My Power's coming—" He goes into a faith healer routine rolling his eyes and frothing at the mouth—"And I got millions and millions and millions of images of Me, Me, Me, meee." (He nods out—He snaps back into focus screaming and spitting at Uranian Willy.) "You hick—You rat—Called the fuzz on me—All right—(Nods out)—I'm finished but you're still a lousy fink—"

"Address your remarks to me," said the D.S.

"All right you hick sheriffs—I'll cook you all down to decorticated canine preparations—You'll never get the apomorphine formulae in time—Never! Never! Never!" —(Caustic white hot saliva drips from his teeth—A smell of phosphorous fills the room)—"Human dogs"— He collapses sobbing—"Don't mind if I take another shot do you?"

"Of course not—After giving information you will be disintoxicated."

"Disintoxicated he says—My God look at me."

"Good sir to the purpose."

"Shit—Uranian shit—That's what my human dogs eat—And I like to rub their nose in it—Beauty—Poetry —Space—What good is all that to me? If I don't get the image fix I'm in the ovens—You understand?—All the pain and hate images come loose—You understand *that* you dumb hick? I'm finished but your eyes still pop out— Naked candy of adolescent image Panama—*Who* look out different?—Cook you all down to decorticated mandrake—"

"Don't you think, Mr. D, it is in your interest to facilitate our work with the apomorphine formulae?"

"It wouldn't touch me—Not with the habit I got—"

"How do you know?—Have you tried?"

"Of course not—If I allowed anyone to develop the formulae he would be *out* you understand?—And it only takes one out to kick over my hypo tray."

"After all you don't have much choice Mr. D."

Again the image snapped back fading now and flickering like an old film—

"I still have the Board Room Reports—I can split the planet wide open tomorrow—And you, you little rat, you'll end up on ice in the ovens—Baked Alaska we call it—Nothing like a Baked Alaska to hold me vegetable— Always plenty wise guys waiting on the Baked Alaska." The dwarf's eyes sputtered blue sparks—A reek of burning flesh billowed through the room—

"I still mushroom planet wide open for jolly—Any hick poet shit out pleasures—Come closer and see my pictures—Show you something interesting—Come closer and watch them flop around in soiled linen—The Garden Boys both of us good as we used to be—Sweet pictures

start coming in the hanged man knees up to the chin—
You know—Beauty bare and still as good—Cock stand
up spurting whitewash—Ever try his crotch when the egg
cracks?—Now I got all the images in backward time—
Rusty black pants—Delicate gooks in the locker room
rubbing each other—I got screams—I *watched*—Burning
heavens, idiot—Don't mind if I take another shot—Jimmy
Sheffield is still as good as he used to be—Flesh the room
in pink carnival—"

A young agent turned away vomiting; "Police work
is not pleasant on any level," said the D.S. He turned
to Winkhorst: "This special breed spitting notice on your
dirty pharmaceuticals—Level—"

"Well some of my information was advantage—It *is*
done with a cyclotron—But like this—Say I want to heat
up the mescaline formula what I do is put the blazing
photo from Hiroshima and Nagasaki under my cyclotron
and shade the heat meal in with mescaline—Indetectible—
It's all so simple and magnificent really—Beauty bare and
all that—Or say I want 'The Drenched Lands' on the boy
what I do is put the image from his cock under the
cyclotron spurting whitewash in the white hot skies of
Minraud."

The death dwarf opens one eye—"Hey, copper, come
here—Got something else to tell you—Might as well rat—
Everyone does it here the man says—You know about
niggers? Why darkies were born?—Travel flesh we call it
—Transports better—Tell you something else—" He nods
out.

"And the apomorphine formula, Mr. Winkhorst?"

"Apomorphine is no word and no image—It is of course
misleading to speak of a silence virus or an apomorphine
virus since apomorphine is anti-virus—The uh apomorphine preparations must be raised in a culture containing
sublethal quantities of pain and pleasure cyclotron con-

centrates—Sub-virus stimulates anti-virus special group—
When immunity has been established in the surviving
preparations—and many will not survive—we have the
formulae necessary to defeat the virus powers—It is simply
a question of putting through an inoculation program in
the very limited time that remains—Word begets image
and image *is* virus—Our facilities are at your disposal
gentlemen and I am at your disposal—Technical sergeant
I can work for anybody—These officers don't even know
what button to push." He glares at the dwarf who is on
the nod, hands turning to vines—

"I'm not taking any rap for a decorticated turnip—
And you just let me tell you how much all the kids in the
office and the laboratory hate you stinking heavy metal
assed cunt sucking board bastards."

Technical Deposition of the Virus Power. "Gentlemen, it
was first suggested that we take our own image and examine
how it could be made more portable. We found that simple
binary coding systems were enough to contain the entire
image however they required a large amount of storage
space until it was found that the binary information could
be written at the molecular level, and our entire image
could be contained within a grain of sand. However it was
found that these information molecules were not dead matter but exhibited a capacity for life which is found else-
where in the form of virus. Our virus infects the human
and creates our image in him.

"We first took our image and put it into code. A technical
code developed by the information theorists. This code was
written at the molecular level to save space, when it was
found that the image material was not dead matter, but exhibited the same life cycle as the virus. This virus released
upon the world would infect the entire population and turn
them into our replicas, it was not safe to release the virus
until we could be sure that the last groups to go replica
would not notice. To this end we invented variety in many
forms, variety that is of information content in a molecule,
which, *enfin,* is always a permutation of the existing ma-

terial. Information speeded up, slowed down, permutated, changed at random by radiating the virus material with high energy rays from cyclotrons, in short we have created an infinity of variety at the information level, sufficient to keep so-called scientists busy for ever exploring the 'richness of nature.'

"It was important all this time that the possibility of a human ever conceiving of being without a body should not arise. Remember that the variety we invented was permutation of the electromagnetic structure of matter energy interactions which are not the raw material of nonbody experience."

Note From The Technical Department of Nova Police: Winkhorst's information on the so-called "apomorphine formulae" was incomplete—He did not mention alnorphine —This substance like apomorphine is made from morphine Its action is to block morphine out of the cells—An injection of alnorphine will bring on immediate withdrawal symptoms in an addict—It is also a specific in acute morphine poisoning—Doctor Isbell of Lexington states in an article recently published in *The British Journal of Addiction* that alnorphine is not habit-forming but acts even more effectively as a pain killer than morphine but can not be used because it produces "mental disturbances"—What is pain?—Obviously damage to the image—Junk is concentrated image and this accounts for its pain killing action—Nor could there be pain if there was no image—This may well account for the pain killing action of alnorphine and also for the unspecified "mental disturbances"—So we began our experiments by administering alnorphine in combination with apomorphine.

Coordinate Points

The case I have just related will show you something of our methods and the people with whom we are called upon to deal.

"I doubt if any of you on this copy planet have ever

seen a nova criminal—(they take considerable pains to mask their operations) and I am sure none of you have ever seen a nova police officer—When disorder on any planet reaches a certain point the regulating instance scans POLICE—Otherwise—SPUT—Another planet bites the cosmic dust—I will now explain something of the mechanisms and techniques of nova which are always deliberately manipulated—I am quite well aware that no one on any planet likes to see a police officer so let me emphasize in passing that the nova police have no intention of remaining after their work is done—That is, when the danger of nova is removed from this planet we will move on to other assignments—We do our work and go—The difference between this department and the parasitic excrescence that often travels under the name 'Police' can be expressed in metabolic terms: The distinction between morphine and apomorphine. 'Apomorphine is made by boiling morphine with hydrochloric acid. This alters chemical formulae and physiological effects. Apomorphine has no sedative narcotic or addicting properties. It is a metabolic regulator that need not be continued when its work is done. I quote from *Anxiety and Its Treatment* by Doctor John Dent of London: 'Apomorphine acts on the back brain stimulating the regulating centers in such a way as to normalize the metabolism.' It has been used in the treatment of alcoholics and drug addicts and normalizes metabolism in such a way as to remove the need for any narcotic substance. Apomorphine cuts drug lines from the brain. Poison of dead sun fading in smoke—"

The Nova Police can be compared to apomorphine, a regulating instance that need not continue and has no intention of continuing after its work is done. Any man who is doing a job is working to make himself obsolete and that goes double for police.

Now look at the parasitic police of morphine. First they create a narcotic problem then they say that a permanent narcotics police is now necessary to deal with the problem of addiction. Addiction can be controlled by apomorphine and reduced to a minor health problem. The narcotics police know this and that is why they do not want to see apomorphine used in the treatment of drug addicts:

PLAN DRUG ADDICTION

Now you are asking me whether I want to perpetuate a narcotics problem and I say: "Protect the disease. Must be made criminal protecting society from the disease."

The problem scheduled in the United States the use of jail, former narcotics plan, addiction and crime for many years—Broad front "Care" of welfare agencies—Narcotics which antedate the use of drugs—The fact is noteworthy—48 stages—prisoner was delayed—has been separated—was required—

Addiction in some form is the basis—must be wholly addicts—Any voluntary capacity subversion of The Will Capital And Treasury Bank—Infection dedicated to traffic in exchange narcotics demonstrated a Typhoid Mary who will spread narcotics problem to the United Kingdom —Finally in view of the cure—cure of the social problem and as such dangerous to society—

Maintaining addict cancers to our profit—pernicious personal contact—Market increase—Release the Prosecutor to try any holes—Cut Up Fighting Drug Addiction by Malcolm Monroe Former Prosecutor, in *Western World*, October 1959.

As we have seen image *is* junk—When a patient loses a leg what has been damaged?—Obviously his image of himself—So he needs a shot of cooked down image—The hallucinogen drugs shift the scanning pattern of "reality" so that we see a different "reality"—There is no true or real "reality"—"Reality" is simply a more or less constant scanning pattern—The scanning pattern we accept as "reality" has been imposed by the controlling power on this planet, a power primarily oriented towards total control—In order to retain control they have moved to monopolize and deactivate the hallucinogen drugs by effecting noxious alterations on a molecular level—

The basic nova mechanism is very simple: Always create as many insoluble conflicts as possible and always aggravate existing conflicts—This is done by dumping life forms with incompatible conditions of existence on the same planet—There is of course nothing "wrong" about any given life form since "wrong" only has reference to conflicts with other life forms—The point is these forms should not be on the same planet—Their conditions of life are basically incompatible in present time form and it is precisely the work of the Nova Mob to see that they remain in present time form, to create and aggravate the conflicts that lead to the explosion of a planet that is to nova—At any given time recording devices fix the nature of absolute need and dictate the use of total weapons— Like this: Take two opposed pressure groups—Record the most violent and threatening statements of group one with regard to group two and play back to group two—Record the answer and take it back to group one—Back and forth between opposed pressure groups—This process is known as "feed back"—You can see it operating in any bar room quarrel—In any quarrel for that matter—Manipulated on a global scale feeds back nuclear war and nova—These conflicts are deliberately created and aggravated by nova criminals—The Nova Mob: "Sammy The Butcher," "Green Tony," "Iron Claws," "The Brown Artist," "Jacky Blue Note," "Limestone John," "Izzy The Push," "Hamburger Mary," "Paddy The Sting," "The Subliminal Kid," "The Blue Dinosaur," and "Mr. & Mrs. D," also known as Mr. Bradly Mr. Martin" also known as "The Ugly Spirit" thought to be the leader of the mob—The Nova Mob—In all my experience as a police officer I have never seen such total fear and degradation on any planet—We intend to arrest these criminals and turn them over to the Biological Department for the indicated alterations—

Now you may well ask whether we can straighten out this mess to the satisfaction of any life forms involved and my answer is this—Your earth case must be processed by the Biologic Courts—admittedly in a deplorable condition at this time—No sooner set up than immediately corrupted so that they convene every day in a different location like floating dice games, constantly swept away by stampeding forms all idiotically glorifying their stupid ways of life—(most of them quite unworkable of course) attempting to seduce the judges into Venusian sex practices, drug the court officials, and intimidate the entire audience chambers with the threat of nova—In all my experience as a police officer I have never seen such total fear of the indicated alterations on any planet—A thankless job you see and we only do it so it won't have to be done some place else under even more difficult circumstances—

The success of the nova mob depended on a blockade of the planet that allowed them to operate with impunity —This blockade was broken by partisan activity directed from the planet Saturn that cut the control lines of word and image laid down by the nova mob—So we moved in our agents and started to work keeping always in close touch with the partisans—The selection of local personnel posed a most difficult problem—Frankly we found that most existing police agencies were hopelessly corrupt— the nova mob had seen to that—Paradoxically some of our best agents were recruited from the ranks of those who are called criminals on this planet—In many instances we had to use agents inexperienced in police work—There were of course casualties and fuck ups—You must understand that an undercover agent witnesses the most execrable cruelties while he waits helpless to intervene—sometimes for many years—before he can make a definitive arrest—

So it is no wonder that green officers occasionally slip control when they finally do move in for the arrest—This condition, known as "arrest fever," can upset an entire operation—In one recent case, our man in Tangier suffered an attack of "arrest fever" and detained everyone on his view screen including some of our own undercover men— He was transferred to paper work in another area—

Let me explain *how* we make an arrest—Nova criminals are not three-dimensional organisms—(though they are quite definite organisms as we shall see) but they need three-dimensional human agents to operate—The point at which the criminal controller intersects a three-dimensional human agent is known as "a co-ordinate point"—And if there is one thing that carries over from one human host to another and establishes identity of the controller it is *habit:* idiosyncrasies, vices, food preferences—(we were able to trace Hamburger Mary through her fondness for peanut butter) a gesture, a certain smile, a special look, that is to say the *style* of the controller—A chain smoker will always operate through chain smokers, an addict through addicts—Now a single controller can operate through thousands of human agents, but he must have a line of coordinate points—Some move on junk lines through addicts of the earth, others move on lines of certain sexual practices and so forth—It is only when we can block the controller out of all coordinate points available to him and flush him out from host cover that we can make a definitive arrest—Otherwise the criminal escapes to other coordinates—

We picked up our first coordinate points in London.

Fade out to a shabby hotel near Earl's Court in London. One of our agents is posing as a writer. He has written a so-called pornographic novel called Naked Lunch in which The Orgasm Death Gimmick is described. That was the bait. And they walked right in. A quick knock at the door and there It was. A green boy/girl from the sewage deltas of Venus. The colorless vampire creatures from a land of grass without mirrors. The agent shuddered in a light fever. "Arrest Fever." The Green Boy mistook this emotion as a tribute to his personal attractions preened himself and strutted round the room. This organism is only dangerous when directed by The Insect Brain Of Minraud. That night the agent sent in his report:

"Controller is woman—Probably Italian—Picked up a villa outside Florence—And a Broker operating in the same area—Concentrate patrols—Contact local partisans —Expect to encounter Venusian weapons—"

In the months that followed we turned up more and more coordinate points. We put a round-the-clock shadow on The Green Boy and traced all incoming and outgoing calls. We picked up The Broker's Other Half in Tangier.

A Broker is someone who arranges criminal jobs:

"Get that writer—that scientist—this artist—He is too close—Bribe—Con—Intimidate—Take over his coordinate points—"

And the Broker finds someone to do the job like: "Call 'Izzy The Push,' this is a defenestration bit—Call 'Green Tony,' he will fall for the sweet con—As a last resort call 'Sammy The Butcher' and warm up The Ovens—This is a special case—"

All Brokers have three-dimensional underworld contacts and rely on The Nova Guards to block shadows and screen their operations. But when we located The Other Half in Tangier we were able to monitor the calls that went back and forth between them.

At this point we got a real break in the form of a defector from The Nova Mob: Uranian Willy The Heavy Metal Kid. Now known as "Willy The Fink" to his former associates. Willy had long been put on the "unreliable" list and marked for "Total Disposal In The Ovens." But he provided himself with a stash of apomorphine so escaped and contacted our Tangier agent. Fade out.

Uranian Willy

Uranian Willy The Heavy Metal Kid. Also known as Willy The Rat. He wised up the marks. His metal face moved in a slow smile as he heard the twittering supersonic threats through antennae embedded in his translucent skull.

"Death in The Ovens."

"Death in Centipede."

Trapped in this dead whistle stop, surrounded by The Nova Guard, he still gave himself better than even chance on a crash out. Electrician in gasoline crack of history. His brain seared by white hot blasts. One hope left in the universe; Plan D.

He was not out of The Security Compound by a long way but he had rubbed off the word shackles and sounded the alarm to shattered male forces of the earth:

THIS IS WAR TO EXTERMINATION. FIGHT CELL BY CELL THROUGH BODIES AND MIND SCREENS OF THE EARTH. SOULS ROTTEN FROM THE ORGASM DRUG, FLESH SHUDDERING FROM THE OVENS, PRISONERS OF THE EARTH COME OUT. STORM THE STUDIO—

Plan D called for Total Exposure. Wise up all the marks everywhere. Show them the rigged wheel of Life-Time-Fortune. Storm The Reality Studio. And retake the universe. The Plan shifted and reformed as reports came in from his electric patrols sniffing quivering down streets and mind screens of the earth.

"Area mined—Guards everywhere—Can't quite get through—"

"Order total weapons—Release Silence Virus—"

"Board Books taken—Heavy losses—"

"Photo falling—Word falling—Break Through in Grey Room—Use Partisans of all nations—*Towers, open fire—*"

The Reality Film giving and buckling like a bulkhead under pressure and the pressure gauge went up and up. The needle was edging to NOVA. Minutes to go. Burnt metal smell of interplanetary war in the raw noon streets swept by screaming glass blizzards of enemy flak. He dispersed on grey sliding between light and shadow down mirror streets and shadow pools. Yes he was wising up the marks. Willy The Fink they called him among other things, syndicates of the universe feeling for him with distant fingers of murder. He stopped in for a cup of "Real English Tea Made Here" and a thin grey man sat at his table with inflexible authority.

"Nova Police. Yes I think we can quash the old Nova Warrants. Work with us. We want names and coordinate points. Your application for Biologic Transfer will have to go through channels and is no concern of this department. Now we'll have a look at your room if you don't mind." They went through his photos and papers with fingers light and cold as spring wind. Grey Police of The Regulator, calm and grey with inflexible authority. Willy had worked with them before. He knew they were undercover agents working under conditions as dangerous as his own. They were dedicated men and would sacrifice him or any other agent to arrest The Nova Mob:

"Sammy The Butcher," "Green Tony," "Iron Claws," "The Brown Artist," "Jacky Blue Note," "Limestone John," "Izzy The Push," "Hamburger Mary," "The Subliminal Kid," "The Green Octopus," and "Willy The Rat," who wised up the marks on the last pitch. And they took Uranus apart in a fissure flash of metal rage.

As he walked past The Sargasso Café black insect flak of Minraud stabbed at his vitality centers. Two Lesbian Agents with glazed faces of grafted penis flesh sat sipping spinal fluid through alabaster straws. He threw up a Silence Screen and grey fog drifted through the café. The deadly Silence Virus. Coating word patterns. Stopping abdominal breathing holes of The Insect People Of Minraud.

The grey smoke drifted the grey that stops shift cut tangle they breathe medium the word cut shift patterns words cut the insect tangle · cut shift that coats word cut breath silence shift abdominal cut tangle stop word holes.

He did not stop or turn around. Never look back. He had been a professional killer so long he did not remember anything else. Uranian born of Nova Conditions. You have to be free to remember and he was under sentence of death in Maximum Security Birth Death Universe. So he sounded the words that end "Word"—
Eye take back color from "word"—
Word dust everywhere now like soiled stucco on the buildings. Word dust without color drifting smoke streets. Explosive bio advance out of space to neon.

At the bottom of the stairs Uranian Willy engaged an Oven Guard. His flesh shrank feeling insect claws under the terrible dry heat. Trapped, cut off in that soulless place. Prisoner eaten alive by white hot ants. With a split second to spare he threw his silver blast and caught the nitrous fumes of burning film as he walked through the door where the guard had stood.

"Shift linguals—Free doorways—Cut word lines— Photo falling—Word falling—Break Through in Grey Room—Use partisans of all nations—*Towers, open fire—*"

Will Hollywood Never Learn?

"Word falling—Photo falling—Break through in Grey Room—"

Insane orders and counter orders issue from berserk Time Machine—

"Terminal electric voice of C—Shift word lines—Vibrate 'tourists.' "

"I said The Chief of Police skinned alive in Baghdad not Washington D.C."

"British Prime Minister assassinated in rightist coup."

"Switzerland freezes all foreign assets—"

"Mindless idiot you have liquidated the Commissar—"

"Cut word lines—Shift linguals—"

Electric storms of violence sweep the planet—Desperate position and advantage precariously held—Governments fall with a whole civilization and ruling class into streets of total fear—Leaders turn on image rays to flood the world with replicas—Swept out by counter image—

"Word falling—Photo falling—Pinball led streets."

Gongs of violence and how—Show you something—Berserk machine—"Mr. Bradly Mr. Martin" charges in with his army of short-time hype artists and takes over The Reality Concession to set up Secretary Of State For Ruined Toilet—Workers paid off in SOS—The Greys came in on a London Particular—SOS Governments fade in worn metal dawn swept out through other flesh—Counter orders issued to the sound of gongs—Machine force of riot police at the outskirts D.C.—Death Dwarfs talking in supersonic blasts of Morse Code—Swept into orbit of the Saturn Galaxy high on ammonia—Time and place shift in speed-up movie—

"Attack position over instrument like pinball—Towers, open fire—"

Atmosphere and climate shifted daily from carbon dioxide to ammonia to pure oxygen—from the dry heat of Minraud to the blue cold of Uranus—One day the natives forced into heavy reptile forms of overwhelming gravity—next floated in tenuous air of plaintive lost planets—Subway broke out every language—D took pictures of a

million battle fields—"Will Hollywood never learn?—
Unimaginable and downright stupid disaster—"

Incredible forms of total survival emerged clashed exploded in altered pressure—Desperate flesh from short
time artists—Transparent civilizations went out talking—

"Death, Johnny, come and took over."

Bradly and I supported by unusual mucus—Stale streets
of yesterday precariously held—Paths of desperate position—Shifting reality—Total survival in altered pressure
—Flesh sheets dissolving amid vast ruins of berserk
machine—"SOS ... ———— ... Coughing enemy
faces—"

"Orbit Sammy and the boys in Silent Space—Carbon
dioxide work this machine—Terminal electric voice of C
—All Ling door out of agitated—"

What precariously held government came over the air—
Total fear in Hicksville—Secretary Of State For Far
Eastern Hotel Affairs assassinated at outskirts of the hotel
—Death Diplomats of Morse code supported in a cocktail
lounge—

"Oxygen Law no cure for widespread blue cold." The
Soviet Union said: "The very people who condemn altered
pressure remain silent—"

Displacement into orbit processes—The Children's
Fund has tenuous thin air of lost places—Sweet Home
Movement to flood it with replicas—

So sitting with my hat on said: "I'm not going to do
anything like that—"

Disgusting death by unusual mucus swept into orbit of
cosmic vomit—(Tenuous candlelight—Remember I was
carbon dioxide)—Rousing rendition of shifting reality—
John lost in about 5000 men and women—Everyone else is
on The Grey Veil—Flesh frozen to particles called "Good
Consciousness" irrevocably committed to the toilet—Colorless slides in Mexican people—Other feature of the code
on Grey Veil—To be read so to speak naked—Have to

do it in dirty pictures—Reverse instructions on car seat—

"Mindless idiot you have liquidated The Shadow Cabinet—"

Swept out tiny police in supersonic Morse code—Emergency Meeting at entrance to the avenue—

"Calling partisans of all nations—Cut word lines—Shift linguals—Vibrate tourists—Free doorways—Word falling—Photo falling—Break through in Grey Room—

—— —— ... ——— .— ... —— ——— ... .

.—— . —— .— —— .. ——— — —— .— —— ... ——— ——

—— —— —— ..— .— —— —— . ... ——.— . — —— ."

Towers Open Fire

Concentrate Partisans—Take Towers in Spanish Villa—Hill 32—The Green Airborne poured into the garden—Lens googles stuttering light flak—Antennae guns stabbing strafing The Vampire Guards—They pushed the fading bodies aside and occupied The Towers—The Technician twirled control knobs—He drank a bicarbonate of soda and belched into his hand—*Urp.*

"God damned captain's a brown artist—Uranus is right—What the fuck kind of a set is this—?? Not worth a fart—Where's the reverse switch? Found it—Come in please—*Urp Urp Urp.*"

"Target Orgasm Ray Installations—Gothenberg Freelandt—Coordinates 8 2 7 6—Take Studio—Take Board Books—Take Death Dwarfs—"

Supersonic sex pictures flickered on the view screen—The pilots poised quivering electric dogs—Antennae light guns twisting searching feeling enemy nerve centers—

"*Focus.*"

"*Did it.*"

"*Towers, open fire—*"

Strafe—Pound—Blast—Tilt—Stab—*Kill*—Air Hammers on their Stone Books—Bleep Bleep Bleep—*Death to The Nova Guard—Death to The Vampire Guards—*
Pilot K9 blasted The Scorpion Guards and led Break Through in Grey Room—Place Of the Board Books And The Death Dwarfs—A vast grey warehouse of wire mesh cubicles—Tier on tier of larval dwarfs tube-fed in bottles —The Death Dwarfs Of Minraud—Operation Total Disposal—Foetal dwarfs stirred slowly in green fluid fed through a tube in the navel—Bodies compacted layer on layer of transparent sheets on which was written The Message Of Total Disposal when the host egg cracks— Death Dwarfs waiting transfer to The Human Host— Written on The Soft Typewriter from The Stone Tablets of Minraud—

"Break Through in Grey Room—Death Dwarfs taken —Board Books taken—"

"Proceed to Sex Device and Blue Movie Studio— Behind Book Shop—Canal Five at Spiegel Bridge—"

"Advancing on Studio—Electric storms—Can't quite get through—"

"Pilot K9, you are hit—back—down"
The medics turned drum music full blast through his head phones—"Apomorphine on the double"—Frequency scalpel sewing wounds with wire photo polka dots from The Image Bank—In three minutes K9 was back in combat driving pounding into a wall of black insect flak—The Enemy Installation went up in searing white blast—Area of combat extended through the vast suburban concentration camps of England and America—Screaming Vampire Guards caught in stabbing stuttering light blast—

"Partisans of all nations, open fire—tilt—blast—pound —stab—strafe—kill—"

"Pilot K9, you are cut off—back. Back. Back before the whole fucking shit house goes up—Return to base immediately—Ride music beam back to base—Stay out

of that time flak—All pilots ride Pan pipes back to base—"

The Technician mixed a bicarbonate of soda surveying the havoc on his view screen—It was impossible to estimate the damage—Anything put out up till now is like pulling a figure out of the air—Installations shattered—Personnel decimated—Board Books destroyed—Electric waves of resistance sweeping through mind screens of the earth—The message of Total Resistance on short wave of the world—*This is war to extermination—Shift linguals —Cut word lines—Vibrate tourists—Free doorways— Photo falling—Word falling—Break through in grey room —Calling Partisans of all nations—Towers, open fire—"*

CRAB NEBULA

THEY DO NOT HAVE what they call "emotion's oxygen" in the atmosphere. The medium in which animal life breathes is not in that soulless place—Yellow plains under white hot blue sky—Metal cities controlled by The Elders who arc heads in bottles—Fastest brains preserved forever—Only form of immortality open to The Insect People of Minraud—An intricate bureaucracy wired to the control brains directs all movement—Even so there is a devious underground operating through telepathic misdirection and camouflage—The partisans make recordings ahead in time and leave the recordings to be picked up by control stations while they are free for a few seconds to organize underground activities—Largely the underground is made up of adventurers who intend to outthink and displace the present heads—There has been one revolution in the history of Minraud—Purges are constant—Fallen heads destroyed in The Ovens and replaced with others faster and sharper to evolve more total weapons—The principal weapon of Minraud is of course heat—In the center of all their cities stand The Ovens where those who

disobey the control brains are brought for total disposal
—A conical structure of iridescent metal shimmering heat
from the molten core of a planet where lead melts at noon
—The Brass And Copper Streets surround The Oven—
Here the tinkers and smiths work pounding out metal
rhythms as prisoners and criminals are led to Disposal—
The Oven Guards are red crustacean men with eyes like
the white hot sky—Through contact with oven pain and
captured enemies they sometimes mutate to breathe in
emotions—They often help prisoners to escape and a few
have escaped with the prisoners—

(When K9 entered the apartment he felt the suffoca-
tion of Minraud crushing his chest stopping his thoughts—
He turned on reserve ate dinner and carried conversation—
When he left the host walked out with him down the
streets of Minraud past the ovens empty and cold now
—calm dry mind of the guide beside him came to the
corner of 14th and Third—

"I must go back now," said the guide—"Otherwise it
will be too far to go alone."

He smiled and held out his hand fading in the alien
air—)

K9 was brought to the ovens by red guards in white and
gold robe of office through the Brass and Copper Street
under pounding metal hammers—The oven heat drying up
life source as white hot metal lattice closed around him—

"Second exposure—Time three point five," said the
guard—

K9 walked out into The Brass And Copper Streets—
A slum area of vending booths and smouldering slag
heaps crossed by paths worn deep in phosphorescent metal
—In a square littered with black bones he encountered
a group of five scorpion men—Faces of transparent pink
cartilage burning inside—stinger dripping the oven poison
—Their eyes flared with electric hate and they slithered

forward to surround him but drew back at sight of the guard—

They walked on into an area of tattoo booths and sex parlors—A music like wind through fine metal wires bringing a measure of relief from the terrible dry heat—Black beetle musicians saw this music out of the air swept by continual hot winds from plains that surround the city—The plains are dotted with villages of conical paper-thin metal houses where a patient gentle crab people live unmolested in the hottest regions of the planet—

Controller of the Crab Nebula on a slag heap of smouldering metal under the white hot sky channels all his pain into control thinking—He is protected by heat and crab guards and the brains armed now with The Blazing Photo from Hiroshima and Nagasaki—The brains under his control are encased in a vast structure of steel and crystal spinning thought patterns that control whole galaxies thousand years ahead on the chessboard of virus screens and juxtaposition formulae—

So The Insect People Of Minraud formed an alliance with the Virus Power Of The Vegetable People to occupy planet earth—The gimmick is reverse photosynthesis—The Vegetable People suck up oxygen and all equivalent sustenance of animal life—Always the colorless sheets between you and what you see taste touch smell eat—And these green vegetable junkies slowly using up your oxygen to stay on the nod in carbon dioxide—

When K9 entered the café he felt the colorless smell of the vegetable people closing round him taste and sharpness gone from the food people blurring in slow motion fade out—And there was a whole tank full of vegetable junkies breathing it all in—He clicked some reverse combos through the pinball machine and left the café—In the street citizens were yacking like supersonic dummies—The SOS addicts had sucked up all the silence in the area were now sitting around in blue blocks of heavy metal the earth's crust buckling ominously under their weight—He shrugged: "Who am I to be critical?"

He knew what it meant to kick an SOS habit: White hot agony of thawing metal—And the suffocating panic of carbon dioxide withdrawal—

Virus defined as the three-dimensional coordinate point of a controller—Transparent sheets with virus perforations like punch cards passed through the host on the soft machine feeling for a point of intersection—The virus attack is primarily directed against affective animal life —Virus of rage hate fear ugliness swirling round you waiting for a point of intersection and once in immediately perpetrates in your name some ugly noxious or disgusting act sharply photographed and recorded becomes now part of the virus sheets constantly presented and represented before your mind screen to produce more virus word and image around and around it's all around you the invisible hail of bring down word and image—

What does virus do wherever it can dissolve a hole and find traction?—It starts eating—And what does it do with what it eats?—It makes exact copies of itself that start eating to make more copies that start eating to make more copies that start eating and so forth to the virus power the fear hate virus slowly replaces the host with virus copies —Program empty body—A vast tapeworm of bring down word and image moving through your mind screen always at the same speed on a slow hydraulic-spine axis like the cylinder gimmick in the adding machine—How do you make someone feel stupid?—You present to him all the times he talked and acted and felt stupid again and again any number of times fed into the combo of the soft calculating machine geared to find more and more punch cards and feed in more and more images of stupidity disgust propitiation grief apathy death—The recordings leave electromagnetic patterns—That is any situation that causes rage will magnetize rage patterns and draw around the rage word and image recordings—Or some disgusting sex practice once the connection is made in childhood whenever the patterns are magnetized by sex desire the same word and image will be presented—And so forth—The counter move is very simple—This is machine strategy and the machine can be redirected—Record for ten minutes on a tape recorder—Now run the tape back without playing and cut in other words at random—Where you have cut in and re-recorded words are wiped off the tape and new words in their place—You have turned time back ten minutes and wiped electromagnetic word patterns off the tape and substituted other patterns—You can do the same with mind tape after working with the tape recorder—(This takes some experimentation)—The old mind tapes can be wiped clean—Magnetic word dust falling from old patterns—Word falling—Photo falling—"Last week Robert Kraft of the Mount Wilson and Palomar Observatories reported some answers to the riddle of exploding stars—Invariably he found the exploding star was locked by gravity to a nearby star—The two stars are in a strange symbiotic relationship—One is a small hot blue star—(Mr. Bradly) Its companion is a larger red star—(Mr. Martin)—Because the stellar twins are so close together the blue star continually pulls fuel in the form of hydrogen gas from the red star—The motion of the system spins the hydrogen into an incandescent figure eight—One circle of the eight encloses one star—The other circle encloses the other—supplied with new fuel the blue star ignites."—Quote, *Newsweek,* Feb. 12, 1962—

The Crab Nebula observed by the Chinese in 1054 A.D. is the result of a supernova or exploding star—Situated approximately three thousand light years from the earth—(Like three thousand years in hot claws at the window—You got it?—)—Before they blow up a star they have a spot picked out as many light years away

as possible—Then they start draining all the fuel and
charge to the new pitch and siphon themselves there right
after and on their way rejoicing—You notice we don't
have as much time as people had say a hundred years
ago?—Take your clothes to the laundry write a letter pick
up your mail at American Express and the day is gone—
They are short-timing us as many light years as they can
take for the getaway—It seems that there were survivors
on The Crab Pitch who are not in all respects reasonable
men—And The Nova Law moving in fast—So they start
the same old lark sucking all the charge and air and color
to a new location and then?—*Sput*—You notice something
is sucking all the flavor out of food the pleasure out of
sex the color out of everything in sight?—Precisely creating
the low pressure area that leads to nova—So they move
cross the wounded galaxies always a few light years ahead
of the Nova Heat—That is they did—The earth was our
set—And they walked right into the antibiotic handcuffs—
It will readily be seen that having created one nova they
must make other or answer for the first—I mean three
thousand years in hot claws at the window like a giant
crab in slag heaps of smouldering metal—Also the more
novas the less time between they are running out of
pitches—So they bribe the natives with a promise of
transportation and immortality—

"Yeah, man, flesh and junk and charge stacked up
bank vaults full of it—Three thousand years of flesh—
So we leave the bloody apes behind and on our way
rejoicing right?—It's the only way to live—"

And the smart operators fall for it every fucking time—
Talk about marks—One of our best undercover operators
is known as The Rube—He perfected The Reverse Con—
Comes on honest and straight and the smart operators all
think they are conning him—How could they think otherwise until he slips on the antibiotic handcuffs—

"There's a wise guy born every minute," he says.

"Closing time gentlemen—The stenographer will take your depositions—"

"So why did I try to blow up the planet?—Pea under the shell—Now you see it now you don't—Sky shift to cover the last pitch—Take it all out with us and hit the road—I am made of metal and that metal is radioactive—Radioactivity can be absorbed up to a point but radium clock hands tick away—Time to move on—Only one turnstile—Heavy planet—Travel with Minraud technicians to handle the switchboard and Venusians to make flesh and keep the show on the road—Then The Blazing Photo and we travel on—Word *is* flesh and word *is* two that is the human body is compacted of two organisms and where you have two you have word and word is flesh and when they started tampering with the word that was it and the blockade was broken and The Nova Heat moved in—The Venusians sang first naturally they were in the most immediate danger—They live underwater in the body with an air line—And that air line is the word—Then the technicians spilled and who can blame them after the conditions I assigned to keep them technicians—Like three thousand years in hot claws—So I am alone as always—You understand nova is where I am born in such pain no one else survives in one piece—Born again and again cross the wounded galaxies—I am alone but not what you call 'lonely'—Loneliness is a product of dual mammalian structure—'Loneliness,' 'love,' 'friendship,' all the rest of it—I am not two—I am *one*—But to maintain my state of oneness I need twoness in other life forms—Other must talk so that I can remain silent—If another becomes one then I am two—That makes two ones makes two and I am no longer one—Plenty of room in space you say?—But I am not one in space I am one in time—Metal time—Radioactive time—So of course I tried to keep you all out of space—That is the end of time—And those who were allowed out sometimes for special services like creating a

useful religious concept went always with a Venusian guard
—All the 'mystics' and 'saints'—All except my old enemy
Hassan i Sabbah who wised up the marks to space and
said they could be one and need no guard no other half
no word—

"And now I have something to say to all you angle boys
of the cosmos who thought you had an in with The Big
Operator—'Suckers! Cunts! Marks!—I hate you all—And
I never intended to cut you in or pay you off with anything but horse shit—And you can thank The Rube if you
don't go up with the apes—Is that clear enough or shall I
make it even clearer? You are the suckers cunts marks I
invented to explode this dead whistle stop and go up with
it—' "

A Bad Move

Could give no other information than wind walking in
a rubbish heap to the sky—Solid shadow turned off the
white film of noon heat—Exploded deep in the alley
tortured metal Oz—Look anywhere, Dead hand—Phosphorescent bones—Cold Spring afterbirth of that hospital
—Twinges of amputation—Bread knife in the heart paid
taxi boys—If I knew I'd be glad to look anyplace—No
good myself—Clom Fliday—Diseased wind identity fading
out—Smoke is all—We intersect in the dark mutinous
door—Hairless skull—Flesh smeared—Five times of dust
we made it all—consumed by slow metal fires—Smell of
gasoline envelops last electrician—I woke up with dark
information from the dead—Board Room Reports waiting
for Madrid—Arrested motion con su medicina—Soft
mendicant "William" in the dark street—He stood there
1910 straw words falling—Dead lights and water—Either
way is a bad move—Better than that?—Gone away can
tell you—No good No bueno—White flash mangled silver

eyes—Flesh flakes in the sky—Explosive twinges of amputation—Mendicant the crooked crosses and barren the dark street—No more—No más—Their last end—Wounded galaxies tap on the pane—Hustling myself—Clom Fliday —And one fine tell you—No good—No bueno—

Be cheerful sir our revels touch the sky—The white film made of Mr. Martin—Rotting phosphorescent bones carried a gasoline dream—Hand falling—White flash mangled "Mr. Bradly Mr. Martin"—Thing Police, Board Room Death Smell, time has come for the dark street— No more—No más wounded galaxies—I told him you on aid—Died out down stale streets through convolutions of our ever living poet—On this green land the dollar twisted to light a last cigarette—Last words answer you—

Long time between suns behind—Empty hunger cross the wounded sky—Cold your brain slowly fading—I said by our ever living poet dead—Last words answer your summons—May not refuse vision in setting forth the diary—Mr. Martin Mr. Corso Mr. Beiles Mr. Burroughs now ended—These our actors, William—The razor inside, sir—Jerk the handle—That hospital melted into air— Advance and inherit the insubstantial dead—Flakes fall that were his shadow—

Metal chess determined gasoline fires and smoke in motionless air—Smudge two speeds—DSL walks "here" beside me on extension lead from hairless skull—Flesh-smeared recorder consumed by slow metal fires—Dog-proof room important for our "oxygen" lines—Group respective recorder layout—"Throw the gasoline on them" determined the life form we invaded: insect screams—I woke up with "marked for invasion" recording set to run for as long as phantom "cruelties" are playing back while waiting to pick up Eduardo's "corrupt" speed and volume variation Madrid—Tape recorder banks tumescent flesh— Our mikes planning speaker stood there in 1910 straw word—Either way is a bad move to The Biologic Stair-

way—The whole thing tell you—No good—No bueno
outright or partially—The next state walking in a rubbish
heap to Form A—Form A directs sound channels heat—
White flash mangled down to a form of music—Life
Form A as follows was alien focus—Broken pipes refuse
"oxygen"—Form A parasitic wind identity fading out—
"Word falling—Photo falling" flesh-smeared counter orders
—determined by last Electrician—Alien mucus cough
language learned to keep all Board Room Reports waiting
sound formations—Alien mucus tumescent code train on
Madrid—Convert in "dirty pictures 8"—simple repetition
—Whole could be used as model for a bad move—Better
than shouts: "No good—No bueno"—

"Recorders fix nature of absolute need: *occupy—"Here"*
—Any cruelties answer him—Either unchanged or reverse
—Clang—Sorry—Planet trailing somewhere along here—
Sequential choice—Flesh plots con su medicina—The next
state according to—Stop—Look—Form A directs sound
channels—Well what now?—Final switch if you want to—
Dead on Life Form B by cutting off machine if you want
to—Blood form determined by the switch—Same need—
Same step—Not survive in any "emotion"—Intervention?
—It's no use I tell you—Familiar will be the end product?
—Reciprocate complete wires? You fucking can't—Could
we become part of the array?—In The American Cemetery—Hard to distinguish maps came in at the verbal level
—This he went to Madrid?—And so si learn? The
accused was beyond altered arrival—So?—So mucus machine runs by feeding in over The American—Hear it?—
Paralleled the bell—Hours late—They all went away—
You've thought it out?—A whole replaced history of life
burial tapes being blank?—Could this 'you' 'them' 'whatever' learn? Accused was beyond altered formations—No
good—Machine runs by feeding in 'useless'—Blood spilled
over Grey Veil—Parallel spurt—How many looking at
dirty pictures—? Before London Space Stage tenuous

face maybe—Change—Definite—The disorder gets you model for behavior—Screams?—Laughter?"—Voice fading into advocate:

"Clearly the whole defense must be experiments with two tape recorder mutations."

Again at the window that never was mine—Reflected word scrawled by some boy—Greatest of all waiting lapses—Five years—The ticket exploded in the air—For I dont know—*I do not know* human dreams—Never was mine—Waiting lapse—Caught in the door—Explosive fragrance—Love between light and shadow—The few who lived cross the wounded galaxies—Love?—Five years I grew muttering in the ice—Dead sun reached flesh with its wandering dream—Buried tracks, Mr. Bradly, so complete was the lie—Course—Naturally—Circumstances now Spanish—Hermetic you understand—Locked in her heart of ooze—A great undersea blight—Atlantis along the wind in green neon—The ooze is only colorless question drifted down—Obvious one at that—Its goal?—That's more difficult to tap on the pane—One aspect of virus— An obvious one again—Muttering in the dogs for generalizations—The lice we intersect—Poison of dead sun anywhere else—What was it the old crab man said about the lice?—Parasites on "Mr. Martin"—My ice my perfect ice that never circumstances—Now Spanish cautiously my eyes—And I became the form of a young man standing —My pulse in unison—Never did I know resting place— Wind hand caught in the door—cling—Chocada—to tap on the pane—

Chocada—Again—Muttering in the dogs—Five years —Poison of dead sun with her—With whom?—I dunno —See account of the crooked crosses—And your name?— Berg?—Berg?—Bradly?—"Mr. Martin si" Disaster Snow —Crack—Sahhk—Numb—Just a fluke came in with the tide and The Swedish River of Gothenberg—

The Death Dwarf in the Street

Biologic Agent K9 called for his check and picked up supersonic imitation blasts of The Death Dwarfs—"L'addition — Laddittion — Laddittion — Garcon — Garcon Garcon"—American tourist accent to the Nth power—He ordered another coffee and monitored the café—A whole table of them imitating word forms and spitting back at supersonic speed—Several patrons rolled on the floor in switch fits—These noxious dwarfs can spit out a whole newspaper in ten seconds imitating your words after you and sliding in suggestion insults—That is the entry gimmick of The Death Dwarfs: supersonic imitation and playback so you think it is your own voice— (do you own a voice?) they invade The Right Centers which are The Speech Centers and they are in the right —in the right—in thee write—"RIGHT"—"I'm in the right—in the right—You know I'm in the right so long as you hear me say inside your right centers 'I am in the right' "—While Sex Dwarfs tenderize erogenous holes—So The Venusian Gook Rot flashed round the world—

Agent K9 was with The Biologic Police assigned to bring the Dwarf Plague under control by disconnecting the dwarfs from Central Control Station: The Insect Brain of Minraud enclosed in a crystal cylinder from which run the cold wires to an array of calculating machines feeding instructions to The Death Dwarf In The Street—The brain is surrounded by Crab Guards charged from The Thermodynamic Pain And Energy Bank—Crab Guards can not be attacked directly since they are directly charged by attack—K9 had been in combat with The Crab Guards and he knew what can happen if they get their claws on your nerve centers—

K9 left the café and surveying the street scene he

could not but feel that someone had goofed—The Death
Dwarfs had in many cases been separated from the
human host but they were still charged from Central
Control and yacked through the streets imitating words
and gestures of everyone in sight—While Sex Dwarfs
squirmed out of any cover with a perfunctory, "Hello
there," in anyone who stood still for it, dissolved erogenous holes immediately attacked by The Talk Dwarfs
so that in a few seconds the unfortunate traveler was
torn to pieces which the dwarfs snatch from each
other's mouth with shrill silver screams—In fact the
noxious behavior of this life form harried the citizens
beyond endurance and everyone carried elaborate home-
made contrivances for screening out the Talk Dwarfs and
a special plastic cover to resist erogenous acids of the
Sex Dwarfs—

Without hesitation K9 gave the order: "Release Silence
Virus—Blanket area"—So The Silence Sickness flashed
round the world at speed of light—As a result many
citizens who had been composed entirely of word went
ape straight away and screamed through the streets
attacking the passers-by who in many cases went
ape in turn as The Silence Sickness hit—To combat
these conditions, described as "intolerable," political
leaders projected stern noble image from control towers
and some could occupy and hold up the ape forms
for a few days or weeks—Invariably the leader was
drained by the gravity of unregenerate apes, torn in
pieces by his relapsing constitutents, or went ape himself on TV—So the Survivors as they call themselves
lived in continual dread of resistant dwarfs always
more frantic from host hunger—Knowing that at any
minute the man next to you in the street might go
Mandril and leap your your throat with virginal canines
—K9 shrugged and put in a call for Technicians—"The
error in enemy strategy is now obvious—It is machine

strategy and the machine can be redirected—Have
written connection in The Soft Typewriter the machine
can only repeat your instructions since it can not create
anything—The operation is very technical—Look at a
photomontage—It makes a statement in flexible picture
language—Let us call the statement made by a given
photomontage X—We can use X words X colors X odors
X images and so forth to define the various aspects of
X—Now we feed X into the calculating machine and X
scans out related colors, juxtapositions, affect-charged
images and so forth we can attenuate or concentrate X
by taking out or adding elements and feeding back into
the machine factors we wish to concentrate—A Technician learns to think and write in association blocks
which can then be manipulated according to the laws
of association and juxtaposition—The basic law of association and conditioning is known to college students
even in America: Any object, feeling, odor, word, image
in juxtaposition with any other object feeling, odor,
word or image will be associated with it—Our technicians learn to read newspapers and magazines for juxtaposition statements rather than alleged content—We
express these statements in Juxtaposition Formulae—
The Formulae of course control populations of the
world—Yes it is fairly easy to predict what people will
think see feel and hear a thousand years from now if
you write the Juxtaposition Formulae to be used in that
period—But the technical details you understand and
the machines—all of which contain basic flaws and
must be continually overhauled, checked, altered whole
blocks of computing machines purged and disconnected
from one minute to the next—fast our mind waves and
long counts—And let me take this opportunity of re-
plying to the criticisms of my creeping opponents—It
is not true that I took part in or instigated experiments
defining pain and pleasure thresholds—I used abstract

reports of the experiments to evolve the formulae of pain and pleasure association that control this planet— I assume no more responsibility than a physicist working from material presented to an immobilized brain— I have constructed *a* physics of the human nervous system or more accurately the human nervous system defines the physics I have constructed—Of course I can construct another system working on quite different principles—Pain is a quantitative factor—So is pleasure —I had material from purge trials and concentration camps and reports from Nagasaki and Hiroshima defining the limits of courage—Our most precise data came from Lexington Ky. where the drug addicts of America are processed—The pain of heroin withdrawal in the addict lends itself perfectly to testing under control conditions—Pain is quantitative to degree of addiction and stage of withdrawal and is quantitatively relieved by cell-blanketing agents—With pain and pleasure limits defined and the juxtaposition formulae set up it is fairly easy to predict what people will think in a thousand years or as long as the formulae remain in operation—I can substitute other formulae if I am permitted to do so—No one has given much thought to building a qualitative mathematics—My formulae saw to that—Now here is a calculating machine—Of course it can process qualitative data—Color for example—I feed into the machine a blue photo passes to the Blue Section and a hundred or a thousand blue photos rustle out while the machine plays blues in a blue smell of ozone blue words of all the poets flow out on ticker tape—Or feed in a thousand novels and scan out the last pages—That is quality is it not? Endingness?"

"Green Tony squealed and I'm off for Galaxy X—"

"The whole mob squealed—Now we can move in for some definitive arrests—Set arrest machinery in operation—Cover all agents and associations with juxtaposition formulae—Put out scanning patterns through coordinate points of the earth for Mr. & Mrs. D—Top Nova Criminals—Through mind screens of the earth covering coordinate points blocking D out of a hand a mouth a cold sore—Silver antibiotic handcuffs fitting D virus filters and—Lock—Click—We have made the arrest—You will understand why all concepts of revenge or moral indignation must be excised from a biologic police agent—We are not here to keep this tired old injustice show on the road but to stop it short of Nova—"

"Nova—Nova—Nova—" shriek the Death Dwarfs— "Arrest good kind Mr. D?—Why he paid for my hernia operation—"

"That did it—Release Silence Virus—Blanket Area—"

"Thinking in association blocks instead of words enables the operator to process data with the speed of light on the association line—Certain alterations are of course essential—"

Extremely Small Particles

Dec. 17, 1961—Past Time—The error in enemy strategy is now to be gathered I was not at all close and the machine can be redirected—These youths of image and association now at entrance to the avenue carrying banners of inter language—

Time: The night before adventurers who hope to form another blazing photo—Injury Headquarters Concentration with reports from Hiroshima—Some of the new hallucinogens and Nagasaki—Slight overdose of dimethyltryptamine—Your cities are ovens where South American narcotic plants brought total disposal—Brain screams of millions who have controller lives in that place screamed back from white hot blue sky—Can always pull the nova equipped now with tower blasts from Hiroshima and Nagasaki—In such pain he has only one turnstile—

Bureaucracy tuned in on all—Incredibly devious conditions hatch cosmologies of telepathic misdirection —Mind screen movies overlapping make recordings ahead and leave before thinking was recorded—Our most precise data came from U.N. (United Narcotics)—His plan was drug addicts of America slip through the cordon— Pain of heroin failure often the cause of windows to pursue ends not compatible cell-blanketing agent—Our most precise data with The Silent People—Plan was almost superhuman drug burned through his juxtapositions—He was naked now to Nagasaki defining the limits against him—The projector can shift its succinct army before flesh dissolving—

Integrity and bravery are difficulties in the laboratory—Experiments to evolve ill took control this planet —Through the streets Nagasaki defining the limits of bravery—We find nationalisms and clashings to degree of addiction—It is fairly easy to predict inter police taking arms to protect their own forgeries from the taken over—Might reach 500 Ideology Headquarters armed with Board Officers produced synthetically—The hallucinogen drugs bottle three-dimensional coordinate points—New hallucinogens directed against affective animal life—Slight overdose of ugliness fear and hate—The ovens were image dust swirling round you total disposal—Some ugly noxious disgusting act sharply recorded becomes now part of "Photo falling—Word Falling"—Presented and represented before towers open fire—Alien virus can dissolve millions —It starts eating—Screamed back white hot copies of itself—So the Fear Species can replace the host armed now with tapeworm of bring down word and image plus Nagasaki—Injury Headquarters—Dual mammalian structure—Hiroshima People—Or some disgusting officers produced the rest of it—

Attorney General For Fear announced yesterday the discovery that cries of nepotism might "form a new mineral damaging to the President"—Insidious form of high density silica as extremely small particles got into politics with Lyndon B. Johnson, wife of two Negro secret service men—Another Mineral American formed by meteorite impact—"And it would make a splendid good talker," he said—

At these tables there is virtually jostling diplomats—Some displacements of a sedate and celebrated rose garden but ideal for the processes of a quiet riverview restaurant—Police juice and the law are no cure for widespread public petting in chow lines the Soviet Union said yesterday—Anti-American promptly denounced Kennedy's moribund position of insistence:

"Washington know-how to deal with this sort demonstration in Venezuela of irresponsible propaganda—Outside Caracas I am deeply distressed at the Soviet Union's attempt to drag us back just when we was stoned in violation of the administration's twenty billion dollar solemn word—"

He begged as a personal thing scattered uprisings—

Error in enemy strategy is switchboard redirected—Word is TWO that is the noxious human inter language recorded—And where you have TWO you have odor's and nationalism's word—They started tampering with net—Injury Headquarters blockade was broken—"Calling partisans of all nations—Crab word falling—Virus photo falling—Break through in Grey Room—"

FROM A LAND OF GRASS
WITHOUT MIRRORS

THE CADET stepped out of a jungle of rancid swamp pools covered with spider webs through a slat fence in a place of wooden runways and barriers—walked through a forbidden door and someone said:

"What do you want?"

The cadet looked at the ground and said: "I didn't mean anything."

He walked down a wooden ramp to a school desk of shellacked brown maple where a woman sat.

"Where have you been?"

"I have been to The Far Assembly Meeting—I am on my way back to school—"

"What Assembly Meeting? Where?"

"The Far Assembly Meeting—Over there—"

"That's a lie. The Far Assembly Meeting is in *that* direction."

He composed his face for Basic Pain as he had been

taught to compose his face to show nothing.

"I have been to a meeting," he said.

"You have six hours forced work—Guard—"

And the club crushed into his ribs and kidneys and the sides of his neck jabbed his testicles and stomach no matter how he did or did not do the work assigned and loss of composure was punishable by death. Then taken back to World Trade School K9 and whether he walked fast or slow or between slow and fast more bone-crushing shocks fell through him—So the cadets learn The Basic Formulae of Pain and Fear—Rules and staff change at arbitrary intervals—Cadets encouraged or forced into behavior subject to heaviest sanctions of deprivation, prolonged discomfort, noise, boredom all compensation removed from the offending cadets who were always being shifted from one school to another and never knew if they were succeeding brilliantly or washed out report to disposal—

Lee woke with his spine vibrating and the smell of other cigarette smoke in his room—He walked streets swept by color storms slow motion in spinal fluid came to the fish city of marble streets and copper domes—Along canals of terminal sewage—the green boy-girls tend gardens of pink flesh—Amphibious vampire creatures who breathe in other flesh—double sex sad as the drenched lands of swamp delta to a sky that does not change—Where flesh circulates stale and rotten as the green water —by purple fungoid gills—They breathe in flesh—settling slow in caustic green enzymes dissolving body—eating gills adjusted to the host's breathing rhythm—eat and excrete through purple gills and move in a slow settling cloud of sewage—They are in pairs known as The Other Half— the invisible Siamese twin moving in and out of one body —talk in slow flesh grafts and virus patterns exchanging genital sewage breathe in and out of each other on slow purple gills of half sleep with cruel idiot smiles eating

Terminal Addicts of The Orgasm Drug under a sign cut in black stone:

> The Nature of Begging
> Need?—Lack.
> Want?—Need.
> Life?—Death.

"It is a warning," said The Prince with a slow bronze smile—"We can do no more—Here where flesh circulates like clothes on stale trade flesh of Spain and Forty-Second Street—scanning pattern of legs—pant smell of The Vagrant Ball Players—"

Lee woke with the green breathing rhythm—Gills slow stirring other cigarette smoke in other gills adjusted to the host by color storms—It is in pairs known as The Other Half sweet and rotten they move in and out and talk in spinal fluid exchanging genital sewage on slow purple gills of half sleep—Addicts of The Orgasm Drug —Flesh juice in festering spines of terminal sewage—Run down of Spain and 42nd St. to the fish city of marble flesh grafts—Diseased beggars with cruel idiot smiles eating erogenous holes inject The Green Drug—Sting insect spasms—It is a warning—We can do not—Doesn't change —Even the sky stale and rotten dissolving—

Lee woke in other flesh the lookout different—His body was covered by transparent sheets dissolving in a green mist—

"Lie still—Wait—Flesh frozen still—Deep freeze— Don't move until you can feel arms and legs—Remember in that hospital after spinal anesthesia and tried to get out of bed to my heroin stash and fell-slid all over the floor with legs like blocks of wood."

He moved his head slightly to one side—Rows and tiers of bunks—A dank packing-house smell—Stinging sex nettles lashed his crotch and hot shit exploded down his thigh to the knee—

"Lie still—Wait—"

The sweet rotten smell of diarrhea swept through the air in waves—The Others were moving now—Larval flesh hanging in rags—Faces purple tumescent bursting insect lust rolled in shit and piss and sperm—

"Watch what everyone else is doing and don't do it (—General Orders for Emergency Conditions—)"

He could move his arm now—He reached for his stash of apomorphine and slipped a handful of tablets under his tongue—His body twisted forward and emptied and he jetted free and drifted to the ceiling—Looked down on quivering bodies—crab and centipede forms flashed here and there—Then red swirls of violence—The caustic green mist settled—In a few minutes there was no movement—

Lee was not surprised to see other people he knew— "I brought them with me"—He decided—"We will send out patrols—There must be other survivors"—

He moved cautiously forward the others fanned out on both sides—He found that he could move on his projected image from point to point—He was already accustomed to life without a body—

"Not much different—We are still quite definite and vulnerable organisms"—Certainly being without a body conveyed no release from fear—He looked down—The green mist had formed a carpet of lichen over the bunks and floor of what looked like a vast warehouse—He could see surviving life forms with body—Green creatures with purple fungoid gills—"The atmosphere must be largely carbon dioxide," he decided—He passed a screen through and wiped out all thought and word from the past—He was conversing with his survivors in color flashes and projected concepts—He could feel danger—All around him the familiar fear urgent and quivering—

The two agents sat in basement room 1920 Spanish villa—Rotten spermy insect smell of The Green People swirling in bare corners quivering through boneless substance in color blats—He felt out through the open door on thin music down dark streets swept by enemy patrols and the paralyzing white flak—He moved like an electric dog sniffing pointing enemy personnel and installations through bodies and mind screens of the silent fish city his burning metal eyes Uranian born in the face of Nova Conditions—his brain seared by flash blasts of image war—

In this area of Total Conditions on The Nova Express the agents of shadow empires move on hideous electric needs—Faces of scarred metal back from The Ovens of Minraud—Orgasm Drug addicts back from The Venusian Front—And the cool blue heavy metal addicts of Uranus—

In this area the only reason any agent contacts any other agent is for purpose of assassination—So one assumes that any one close to him or her is there precisely to kill—What else? We never knew anything else here —None the less we are reasonably gregarious since nothing is more dangerous than withdrawing from contact into a dead whistle stop—So every encounter quivers with electric suspicion—ozone smell of invisible flash bulbs—

Agents are always exchanging identities as articles of clothing circulate in strata of hustlers—These exchanges marked by last-minute attempts to switch the package and leave you standing with some old goofball bum in 1910 Panama—Lee had such a deal on with the other agent and of course both were falsifying and concealing defects in the merchandise—Of course no agent will allow a trial run since the borrower would be subject to take off with the package and fuck everybody they'll do it every time— So all the deals are sight unseen both parties gathering what information he can delving into the other identity for hidden miles and engineering flaws that could leave him with faulty equipment in a desperate position—His patrols were checking the other agent—Sending in reports— Conveying instructions—intercepting messages—

"Present Controller is The American Woman—Tracer

on all connections—Taping all lines in and out—Santa Monica California—She is coming in loud and clear now—"

The young man dropped Time on the bed—His face was forming a smooth brown substance like the side of an electric eel—His left hand dissolved in a crystal bulb where a stinger of yellow light quivered sharp as a hypo needle—Orgasm Sting Ray—Venusian weapon—A full dose can tear the body to insect pieces in electric orgasms —Smaller doses bring paralysis and withered limbs of blighted fiber flesh—Lee hummed a little tune and cut the image lines with his grey screen—The Orgasm Sting dissolved in smoke—Lee picked the boy up by one elbow rigid as a clothing dummy and weightless now Lee guided him down the street steering the body with slight movements of the arm—The screen was empty—The boy sat on Lee's bed his face blank as a plate—The Nova police moved in calm and grey with inflexible authority—

" 'Paddy The Sting' arrested—Host empty—Heavy scar tissue—Surgery indicated—Transfer impractical—"

Too Far Down the Road

—The Boy, driven too far down the road by some hideous electric hand—I don't know—Perhaps the boy never existed—All thought and word from the past— It was in the war—I am not sure—You can not know the appalling Venusian Front—Obscure hand taping all messages in and out—Last human contacts—suddenly withdrawn—The Boy had never existed at all—A mouth against the pane—muttering—Dim jerky far away voice: "Know who I am? You come to 'indicated accident' long ago . . . old junky selling Christmas seals on North Clark St. . . . 'The Priest' they called him . . . used to be me, Mister" shabby quarters of a forgotten city . . .

tin can flash flare . . . smell of ashes . . . wind stirs a lock of hair . . . "Know who I am? hock shop kid like mother used to make . . . Wind and Dust is my name . . . Good Bye Mister is my name . . . quiet now . . . I go . . ." (flickering silver smile).

No Good at This Rate

Smell of other cigarette smoke on child track—Proceed to the outer—All marble streets and copper domes inside air—Signature in scar tissue stale and rotten as the green water—Moldy pawn ticket by purple fungoid gills—The invisible Siamese twin moving in through flesh grafts and virus patterns—Exchanging weight on slow purple gills—Addicts of the purpose—Flesh juice vampires is no good—All sewage—Idiot smiles eating erogenous deal—Sweet rotten smell of ice—Insect smell of the green car wreck—The young agent to borrow your body for a special half made no face to conceal the ice—He dies many years ago—He said: "Yes you want to—Right back to a size like that—Said on child track—Screaming on the deal?"

She didn't get it—All possessed by overwhelming inside air—Shoeshine boy, collapse it—Could make or break any place by his male image back in—The shoeshine boy didn't get jump—Wait till the signs are right—And shit sure know to very—Wait a bit—No good—Fast their mind waves and long counts—No use—Don't know the answer—Arsenic two years—Go on treating it—In the blood arsenic and bleeding gums—Now I had my light weight 38 like for protection—

He dies many years ago—"Sunshine of your smile," he said and stomped your ambassador to the mud flats where all died addicted in convulsions of insect—They were addicted to this round of whatever visits of a special kind—

"Grow to a size like that," said Nimum—"So where is my ten percent on the deal?"

The shoeshine boy collapsed and they revived him with secret techniques—The money pinned to an old man's underwear is like that is the best—

So I said: "We can do it here—They won't see us—When I walk with Dib they can't see me—"

Careful—Watch the exits—Don't go to Paris—Wait till the signs are right—Write to everyone—Wait a bit —No good at this rate—Watch the waves and long counts—No use moving out—Try one if you want to— Right back to the track, Jack—Vampires is no good all possessed by overwhelming Minraud girl—All dies in convulsions—Don't go to Paris—Venusian front—On child track screaming without a body—Still quite definite and vulnerable organisms—Nova signature in scar tissue—Purpose of "assassination" back to a size like that —Her is there precisely to kill—Fast their mind waves and attempts to switch the package—Know the answer?: Arsenic two years: Goofball bum in 1910 Panama— They'll do it every time—The young man dropped Time on us with all the Gods of Life—Giggles canal talk from the sewage drifting round the gallows turning cartwheels —Groveled in visits of a special kind—Know the answer?: Arsenic two years: Operation completed—WE are blood arsenic and bleeding gums—

"Are you sure they are not for protection or perhaps too quick?"

"Quite sure—Nothing here but to borrow your body for a special purpose":: ("Excellent—Proceed to the ice")

He dies many years ago—Screen went dead—The smell of gasoline filled straw hat and silk scarf—Won't be much left—Have to move fast—Wouldn't know his

name—No use of them better than they are—You want
to?—Right back to the track, Jack—The Controller at the
exits—

Wind Hand to the Hilt

White sat quietly beaming "humanity's condition"—
Wise Radio Doctor started putting welfare officers in
his portable—The Effects Boys to see if they can do
any locks over the Chinese—Told me to sit down—Gave
me Panorama Comfortable and then said:

"Well? Anything to go by? What are we going to
do?"

What weighted the program down was refusal to leave—

"Well what are you going to do? Perhaps alone?"

"You'd like to do half of it for me would you?"

He slung me out and Worth and Vicky talked usefully
about that was that—Maybe I've met Two Of A Kind—
They both started share of these people—Vicky especially
sounded him—It wasn't what he had—You know is why?
—What they are meant to do is all?—Going to get out of
it?—An interview with Modigliani obvious usually sooner
than later—I've seen a lot of these old men you visit on a
P&O—You know sixty seventy years east voyage—Do
you see yourself ending up in Cathay?—Trying to pinch
suitcase like that you'll end up buying the deluxe straight
—The job will be there—No cleaner—

If you or any of your pals foretold you were all spirits
curtains for them—And trouble for me—Globe is self
you understand until I die—Why do they make soldiers
out of "Mr. Martin?"—Wind hand to the hilt as it is—
work we have to do and the way the flakes fall—Be
trouble in store for me every time—For him always
been and always will be wounded galaxies—We intersect in a strange and crazy bio advance—On the night

shift working with blind—End getting to know whose reports are now ended—These our rotten guts and aching spine accounts—

One more chance he said touching circumstance—Have you still—Come back to the Spanish bait its curtains under his blotter—The square fact is many spirits it's curtains for them—Fed up you understand until I die—No wish to see The Home Secretary "Mr. Martin—"

Wind hand to the hilt—work we have to do and way got the job—Jobbies would like to strike on night shift working the end of hanging—All good thing come to answer Mr. Of The Account screaming for a respectable price—What might be called in air lying about wholesale—*Belt Her*—Find a time buyer before ports are now ended—These are rotten if they start job for instance—Didn't last—Have you still—Come back work was steady at the gate under his blotter—Cover what's left of the window—Do they make soldiers out of present food in The Homicide Act as it is?—Blind bargain in return for accepting "one more chance"—Generous?—Nothing—That far to the bait and it's curtains—End getting to know whose price—Punishment and reward business the bait—No wish to see The Home Secretary "humanity's condition"—Wise radio doctor reprieving officers in his portable got the job—So think before they can do any locks over the Chinese that abolition is war of the past—Jobbies would like to strike a bargain instead of bringing you up fair—The end of hanging generous?—Just the same position—Changed places of years in the end is just the same—What might be called the program was refusal lying about wholesale—Going to do?—Perhaps alone would you?—All good things come to about that was that—Screaming for respectable share of these people —Vicky especially—*Belt her*—Know what they meant if they start job for instance? An interview with further scream along the line—

White sat quietly beaming "human people" out of hospital and others started putting their time on casual —Effects Boys anyway after that—Chinese accusation of a bargain—What are we going to do level on average? —I was on the roof so I had to do Two Of A Kind—They both started before doing sessions—There's no choice— Sounded him—Have to let it go cheap and start do is all —A *journey*, man—The job will be there—No punishment and reward business—

A Distant Thank You

"I am having in Bill&Iam," she said—

"But they don't exist—tout ça—my dear have you any idea what—certain basic flaws in the—"

"You can afford it—You told me hole is always there to absorb yesterday—and whatever—"

"The Market you understand—Bill tossed a rock and a very dear friend of mine struck limestone with dried excrement purposes. And what purpose more has arisen —quite unlooked for—"

"All the more reason to redecorate Silent Workers—" They had arrived where speech is impossible.

"Iam is very technical," said Bill as he walked around smoking smoke patterns in the room—"Have flash language of The Silent Ones—Out all this crap—Tonight, Madame—Age to grim Gothic Foreman—"

The Studio had set up a desert reek Mayan back to peasant hut—In a few minutes there mountain slope of the Andes—House had stood in the air—

"Limestone country," said Bill—"We might start with a photo-collage of The House—yes?—of course and the statues in clear air fell away to a Mayan Ball Court with

eternal gondolas—a terminal life form of bookies and
bettors changing black berries in little jade pipes—slow
ebb of limestone luck and gills—Controllers of The Ugly
Spirit Spinal Fluid—hydraulic vegetable centuries—"

"But what about The House Itself?"

"Lost their enemy—ah yes Madame, The House—You
are Lady—Can't we contact them?—I mean well taken
care of I hope—"

"I think, Bill, they exist at different pressure—"

"Ah yes The House—Hummm—Permutate at different
pressure and sometimes a room is lost in—"

"Bill, they exist at different pressure—"

"In the shuffle?—The Bensons?—But they don't exist
—Tout ça c'est de l'invention—There are of course certain basic flaws in the hydraulic machinery but the marl
hole is always there to absorb the uh errors—"

At the bottom of the crater was a hole—Bill tossed a
rock and the echo fainter and fainter as the rock struck
limestone on down—Silence—

"Bottomless you see for practical purposes—and what
purpose more practical than disposal??"

Slow The House merged created in silent concentration of the workers from The Land Of Silence where
speech is impossible—

"Lucky bastards," Bill always said as he walked around
smoking Havanas and directing the work in color flash
language of The Silent Ones—showing his plans in photo-
collage to grim Gothic foreman—

And The House moved slowly from Inca to Mayan
back to peasant hut in blighted maize fields or windy
mountain slopes of The Andes—Gothic cathedrals soared
and dissolved in air—The walls were made of blocks that
shifted and permutated—cave paintings—Mayan relief
—Attic frieze—panels—screens—photo-collage of The
House in all periods and stages—Greek temples rose in
clear air and fell to limestone huts by a black lagoon

dotted with gondolas—a terminal life form of languid beautiful people smoking black berries in little jade pipes *
—And The Fish People with purple fungoid gills—And The Controllers drifting in translucent envelopes of spinal fluid with slow hydraulic gestures of pressure authority— These people are without weapons—so old they have lost their enemy—

"But they are exquisite," said The Lady. "Can't we contact them?—I mean for dinner or cocktails?—"

"It is not possible, Madame—They exist at different pressure—"

"I am having in Bill&Iam"—she said during breakfast— Her husband went pale—"My dear, have you any idea what their fee is?—"

"You can afford it—You told me only yesterday—"

"That was yesterday and whatever I may have told you in times long past—The Market you understand— Something is happening to money itself—A very dear friend of mine found his *special* deposit box in Switzerland filled with uh dried excrement—In short an emergency a shocking emergency has arisen—quite unlooked-for—"

"All the more reason to redecorate—There they are now—"

They had arrived—Bill in "banker drag he calls it now isn't that cute?"

"Iam is very technical"—said Bill puffing slowly on his Havana and watching smoke patterns—"Have to get some bulldozers in here—clean out all this crap—Tonight, Madame, you sleep in a tent like the Bedouin—"

The Studio had set up a desert on the lawn and The Family was moved out—In a few hours there was only a vast excavation where The House had stood—

---

* Reference to the Pakistan Berries, a small black fruit of narcotic properties sometimes brought to southern Morocco by caravan—when smoked conjures the area of black lagoons sketched in these pages—

"Limestone country," said Bill touching outcrops on walls of the crater—

"We might start with a Mayan temple—or The Greeks—"

"Yes of course and the statuary—City Of Marble Flesh Grafts—I envisage a Mayan Ball Court with eternal youths —and over here the limestone bookmakers and bettors changing position and pedestal—slow ebb of limestone luck —and just here the chess players—one beautiful the other ugly as The Ugly Spirit—playing for beauty—slow game of vegetable centuries—"

"But what about The House itself?"—said The Lady—

"Ah yes, Madame, The House—You are comfortable in your present quarters and well taken care of I hope— I think your son is very talented by the way—Hummm —perhaps—ah yes The House—Gothic Inca Greek Mayan Egyptian—and also something of the archaic limestone hut you understand the rooms and walls permutate on hydraulic hinges and jacks—and sometimes a room is lost in—"

"In the shuffle—The Bensons—during breakfast—"

Her husband went pale—"C'est l'invention—Fee is?"

"Fee is hydraulic machinery marl yesterday errors told you in times long past—at the bottom of the crater was happening to money itself—echo fainter and fainter special deposit box in Switzerland—"

"A shocking emergency—"

"Bottomless you see for practical pee—practical disposal—There they are now—"

Slow the House merged—created in drag he calls it.

"Isn't that cute?—Workers from The Land Of Silence whiffing slowly on his Havana and watching—"

" 'Lucky Bill' always said: 'Get some bulldozers in here.' "

The Family was moved and The House moved slowly —only a vast excavation in blighted maize fields and

wind—Gothic cathedrals soared on walls of the crater
—Blocks shifted relief and panel screens of marble flesh
grafts—

"I envisage stages—Gothic Cathedral soured—And
over here the limestone huts by a black lagoon dotted
position and pedestal—smoke chess players—and Fish
People playing for beauty—slow games in their translucent envelopes—"

"Gestures of Pressure Author—" said The Lady—

"You understand so old they are comfortable in present quarters—"

"But they are exquisite"—said Tower Son—(very
talented by the way for dinner or cocktails Gothic Inca
Mayan Greek Egyptian—and also—)

"You understand the rooms and walls—and sometimes
a room is lost—"

"They exist at different pressure playing their slow
games by The Black Lagoon—You understand the mind
works with une rapidité incroyable but the movements are
very slow—So a player may see on the board great joy
or a terrible fate see also the move to take or avoid see
also that he can not make the move in time—This gives
rise of course to great pain which they must always conceal in a round of exquisite festivals—"

The lagoon now was lighted with flicker lanterns in
color—floating temples pagodas pyramids—

"The festivals rotate from human sacrifice to dawn
innocence when the envelope dissolves—This happens
very rarely—They cultivate The Fish People like orchids
or pearls—always more exquisite strains blending beauty
and vileness—strains of idiot cruelty are specially
prized—" He pointed to a green newt creature with purple
fungoid gills that stirred in a clear pool of water under
limestone outcroppings and ferns—

"This amphibious-hermaphrodite strain is motivated by
torture films—So their attractions are difficult to resist—"

The green boy-girl climbed out on a ledge—A heavy narcotic effluvia drifted from his half open mouth—Her squirmed towards the controller with little chirps and giggles—The controller reached down a translucent hand felt absently into the boneless jelly caressing glands and nerve centers—The green boy-girl twisted in spasms of ingratiation—

"They are very subservient as you can see in the right hands—But we must make an excursion to the place of The Lemur People who die in captivity—They are protected—We are all protected here—Nothing really happens you understand and the human sacrifice takes a bow from the flower floats—It is all exquisite and yet would you believe me we are all intriguing to unload this gold brick on some rube for an exit visa—Oh there's my travel agent the controller engaged—"

Playing their slow games by man in the black suit with long mind—works with une rapidité—

"He has been cheating me for months—slow so that a player may see believe the ridiculous travel arrange great joy and see also the move to fastest brain—"

"Yes we have all—Can not make the move in time—This other here—Roles must conceal in anything to go."

"If we could only just flush our flower floats on child track without a body from human sacrifice—"

"Rather bad taste, Old-Thing-Whose-Envelope-Has-Dissolved—The Flayed Man Stand—"

"They Cultivate The Fish People—"

"Oh yes whose doing it?"

"*Not* for more exquisite strains—??"

"I tell you nobody can scream—Over there is The Land of The Lemur People—"

"He dissolved after the performance—Beautiful strain of idiot cruelty—"

"So he got his exit visa?—and green newt creature with purple fungoid now?"

"Pool of water under limestone—He has contacted someone—Know is motivated by torture films—"

"Willy The Rube?—I knew him to resist—The green boy climbed hook and he fades out with Effluvia—drifted from his half open mouth all our exquisite food and smoke bones—He fade out in word giggles—He beat Green Tony into The Green Boy-Girl's Boneless Dream Concession—He defend nerve centers—The Green Boy twisted in Sammy The Butcher—"

"Still he may fall for The Hero—They are very subservient—"

"We are an old people you are sus—Make an excursion to the land of persona and statuary—They are protected of course—Here is he now—Really happens you understand—"

"I understand you people need the flower floats—It is all Mongolian Archers—They are—we are all scheming to unload an exit visa—" (The controller engaged short furtive conversation—man in a black suit with one long fingernail and gold teeth—)

"He has been cheating me for months of course they all do—You wouldn't believe the ridiculous travel arrangements they unload on our fastest brains—Yes we have all been laughing stock at one time or another—Here where roles and flesh circulate—There is no place for anything to go—"

"If we could only just flush ourselves down the drain," she said seeing her life time fortunes fade on The Invisible Board—

"Rather bad taste, old thing—Embalm yourself—Tonight is The Festival Of The Flayed Man—"

"Oh yes and whose doing it?—Juanito again?—"

"He dissolved after the last performance—"

"Oh yes he went away—And what is The Travel Agent selling you now?"

"He has contacted someone known as Willy the Rube —perhaps—"

"Willy The Rube??—I know him from Uranus—Think you have him on the hook and he fades out with a train whistle—He beat Green Tony in a game of limestone stud and walked out with The Dream Concession—He defenestrated Izzy the Push and cowboyed Sammy The Butcher."

"Still he may fall for The Hero: Protect us—We are an old people—Protect our exquisite poisonous life and our *statuary*—Well?"

"Here is he now."

"I understand you people need protection—I am moving in a contingent of Mongolian Archers—They are expensive of course but well worth it—"

The Mongolian Archers with black metal flesh moved in grill arrangements of a ritual dance flexing their bows —silver antennae arrows sniffing dowsing quivering for The Enemy—

"My dear, they make me terribly nervous—Suppose there is no enemy??"

"That would be unfortunate, Madame—My archers must get relief—You did ask for protection and now— Where are the Lemur People?"

The Lemur People live on islands of swamp cypress peering from the branches and it took many hours to coax them down—Iridescent brown copper color—liquid black eye screens swept by virginal emotions—

"They are all affect you understand—That is why they die in captivity—" A Lemur touched The Rube's face with delicate tentative gestures and skittered again into the branches—

"No one has ever been able to hold a lemur for more than a few minutes in my memory—And it is a thousand years since anyone had intercourse with a lemur— The issue was lost—They are of such a delicacy you understand the least attempt-thought of holding or possessing and they are back in the branches where they wait the master who knew not hold and possess—They have waited a long time—Five hundred thousand years more or less I think—The scientists can never make up their mind about anything—"

The lemur dropped down on Lee's shoulder and playfully nipped his ear—Other lemurs raised sails on a fragile bamboo craft and sailed away over the lagoon under the red satellite that does not change position—

"There are other islands out there where no one has ever been—The lemurs of such delicacy that they die if one sets foot on the island—They exist at different prenatal flesh in black lagoons—"

"You understand silver arrows sniffing pointing incroyable but the movements on The Board a terrible doom: ('Suppose there is no enemy?') Take or avoid but see also that gives rise to great pain—You did a round of exquisite festivals—"

"Me see your lemur people with flicker lights in swamp cypress?"

"Hours to coax them down—Finally the dawn innocence of control sent liquid flickering screens like pearl —All affect, you understand, that is blending beauty and flesh—"

A Lemur touched Lee's face with delicate people who die in captivity—skittering again into the specially prized—this stressing they are back in who will not hold and possess—out on a ledge—a heavy narcotic indeed—thousand years more or less—

The Mongolian Archers with short black conversation of ritual dancing flexed there—dowzing feeling for The Enemy like of course they all do—

"You wouldn't—"

"My dear, they make me terrible arrangements that have been sold to our—"

101

"That would be unfortunate, Madame—Been laughing stock at one time or ask for protection—and now—"

"Tonight is the festival of Nice Young Emotions— Why they die in captivity—Juanito again?—Where is he now?—"

"Branches no one has ever seen—He far now is—"

"They are of such a hat—Is your travel agent selling you attempt or thought of holding the branches where they wait?"

"Perhaps—They have waited a long time—Five Uranus—"

"The Pakistan Berries lay all our dust of a distant thank you on Lee's shoulder—"

Remember I Was Carbon Dioxide

Nothing here now but the recordings—in another country.

"Going to give some riot noises in the old names?"

"Mr. Martin I have survived" (smiles).

"All right young countryman so we took Time . . . Human voices take over my job now . . . Show you around alien darkroom . . . their Gods fading . . . departed file . . . Mrs. Murphy's rooming house left no address. . . . You remember the 'third stair' it was called? You wrote last flight . . . seals on North Beach . . . the lights flashing . . . Clark St. . . . The Priest against a black sky . . . rocks gathered just *here* on this beach . . . Ali *there,* hand lifted . . . dim jerky far away street . . . ash on the water . . . last hands . . . last human voices . . . last rites for Sky Pilot Hector Clark . . . He carries the man who never was back . . . Shall these ticker bones live?? My host had been a long time in inquisition. . . ."

Through all the streets no relief—I will show you fear

on walls and windows people and sky—Wo weilest du?—
Hurry up please its accounts—Empty is the third who
walks beside you—Thin mountain air here and there and
out the window—Put on a clean shirt and dusk through
narrow streets—Whiffs of my Spain from vacant lots—
Brandy neat—April wind revolving lips and pants—After
dinner sleep dreaming on rain—The soldier gives no shelter—War of dead sun is a handful of dust—Thin and
tenuous in gray shivering mist of old Western movies said:
"Fill your hand, Martin."

"I can't, son—Many years ago that image—Remember
I was carbon dioxide—Voices wake us and we drown—Air
holes in the faded film—End of smoky shuttered rooms
—No walls—Look anywhere—No good—Stretching zero
the living and the dead—Five for rain—Young hair too—
Hurry up please its William—I will show you fear in the
cold spring cemetery—Kind, wo weilest du?"

"Here," said she, "is your card: Bread knife in the
heart—"

"What thinking, William?—Were his eyes—Hurry up
please its half your brain slowly fading—Make yourself
a bit smart—It's them couldn't reach flesh—Empty walls
—Good night, sweet ladies—Hurry up please it's time—
Look any place—Faces in the violet light—Damp gusts
bringing rain—"

Got up and fixed in the sick dust—Again he touched
like that—Smell of human love—The tears gathered—
In Mexico committed fornication but—Cold spring—
besides you can say—could give no information—vast
Thing Police—

"What have I my friend to give you?—Identity fading
out—dwindling—Female smells—knife in the heart—
boy of dust gives no shelter—left no address"

"I'd ask alterations but really known them all—Closed
if you wanted a Greek—I do not find The Hanged Man
in the newspapers—blind eyes—see—Who walks beside

you?" "Will you let me tell you lost sight a long time ago
. . . Smell taste dust on the window . . . touch . . . touch??
How should I from remote landing dim jerky far away."

At dawn—Put on a clean shirt in another country—
Soccer scores and KiKi give you?—Empty to the barrier
—Shuttered dawn is far away—Bicycle races here in this
boy were no relief—Long empty noon—Dead recordings
—Moments I could describe that were his eyes in
countries of the world—Left you these sick dawn bodies—
Fading smiles—in other flesh—Far now—Such gives no
shelter—Shifted the visiting address—The wind at noon
—walks beside you?" Piece of a toy revolver there in
nettles of the alley . . . over the empty broken streets a
red white and blue kite.

GAVE PROOF THROUGH THE NIGHT

(*This section, first written in 1938 in collaboration with Kells Elvins who died in 1961, New York, was later cut back in with the "first cut-ups" of Brion Gysin as published in* Minutes to Go.)

CAPTAIN BAIRNS was arrested today in the murder at sea of Chicago—He was The Last Great American to see things from the front and kept laughing during the dark —Fade out

S.S. America—Sea smooth as green glass—off Jersey Coast—An air-conditioned voice floats from microphones and ventilators—:

"Keep your seats everyone—There is no cause for alarm —There has been a little accident in the boiler room but everything is now/"

BLOOOMMM

Explosion splits the boat—The razor inside, sir—He jerked the handle—

A paretic named Perkins screams from his shattered wheelchair:

"You pithyathed thon of a bidth."

Second Class Passenger Barbara Cannon lay naked in First Class State Room—Stewart Hudson stepped to a porthole:

"Put on your clothes, honey," he said. "There's been an accident."

Doctor Benway, Ship's Doctor, drunkenly added two inches to a four-inch incision with one stroke of his scalpel—

"Perhaps the appendix is already out, doctor," the nurse said peering over his shoulder—"I saw a little scar—"

"The appendix *OUT! I'M* taking the appendix out—What do you think I'm doing here?"

"Perhaps the appendix is on the left side, doctor—That happens sometimes you know—"

"Stop breathing down my neck—I'm coming to that—Don't you think I know where an appendix is?—I studied appendectomy in 1910 at Harvard—" He lifted the abdominal wall and searched along the incision dropping ashes from his cigarette—

"And fetch me a new scalpel—This one has no edge to it"—

BLOOOMM

"Sew her up," he ordered—"I can't be expected to work under such conditions"—He swept instruments cocaine and morphine into his satchel and tilted out of The Operating Room—

Mrs. J. L. Bradshinkel, thrown out of bed by the explosion, sat up screaming: "I'm going right back to The Sheraton Carlton Hotel and call the Milwaukee Braves"—

Two Philippine maids hoisted her up—"Fetch my wig, Zalameda," she ordered. "I'm going straight to the captain—"

Mike B. Dweyer, Politician from Clayton, Missouri, charged the First Class Lounge where the orchestra, high on nutmeg, weltered in their instruments—

"Play The Star Spangled Banner," he bellowed.

"You trying to corn somebody, Jack?—We got a union—"

Mike crossed to the jukebox, selected The Star Spangled Banner With Fats Terminal at The Electric Organ, and shoved home a handful of quarters—

Oh say can you seeeeeeeeeee

The Captain sitting opposite Lucy Bradshinkel—He is shifty redhead with a face like blotched bone—

"I own this ship," The Lady said—

The deck tilted and her wig slipped over one ear—The Captain stood up with a revolver in his left hand—He snatched the wig and put it on—

"Give me that kimona," he ordered—

She ran to the porthole screaming for help like everyone else on the boat—Her head was outlined in the porthole—He fired—

"And now you God damned old fool, *give me that kimona*—"

I mean by the dawn's early light

Doctor Benway pushed through a crowd at the rail and boarded The First Life Boat—

"Are you all right?" he said seating himself among the women—"I'm the doctor."

The Captain stepped lightly down red carpeted stairs—In The Purser's Office a narrow-shouldered man was energetically shoving currency and jewels into a black suitcase—The Captain's revolver swung free of his brassiere and he fired twice—

By the rocket's red glare

Radio Operator Finch mixed a bicarbonate of soda and belched into his hand—"SOS—URP—SOS—God damned captain's a brown artist—SOS—Off Jersey Coast

107

—SOS—Might smell us—SOS—Son of a bitching crew—SOS—URP—*Comrade* Finch—SOS—Comrade in a pig's ass—SOS—SOS—SOS—URP—URP—URP—"

The Captain stepped lightly into The Radio Room—Witnesses from a distance observed a roaring blast and a brilliant flash as The Operator was arrested—The Captain shoved the body aside and smashed the apparatus with a chair—

Our flag was still there

The Captain stiff-armed an old lady and filled The First Life Boat—The boat was lowered jerkily by male passengers—Doctor Benway cast off—The crew pulled on the oars—The Captain patted his bulging suitcase absently and looked back at the ship—

Oh say do that star spangled banner yet wave

Time hiccoughs—Passengers fighting around Life Boat K9—It is the last boat that can be launched—Joe Sargant, Third Year Divinity student and MRA, slipped through the crowd and established Perkins in a seat at the bow—Perkins sits there chin drawn back eyes shining clutching a heavy butcher knife in his right hand

By the twilight's last gleamings

Hysterical waves from Second Class flood the deck—"Ladies first," screamed a big face shoe clerk with long teeth—He grabbed a St. Louis matron and shoved her ahead of him—A wedge of shoe clerks formed behind—A shot rang and the matron fell—The wedge scattered—A man with nautical uniform buttoned in the wrong holes carrying a World War I 45 stepped into the last boat and covered the men at the launching ropes—

"Let this thing down," he ordered—The boat hit the water—A cry went up from the reeling deck—Bodies hurtled around the boat—Heads bobbed in the green water

—A hand reached out of the water and closed on the boat side—Spring-like Perkins brought down his knife—The hand slipped away—Finger stubs fell into the boat—Perkins worked feverishly cutting on all sides:

"Bathdarths—Thons of bidth—Bathdarth—thon bidth—Methodith Epithcopal God damn ith—"

O'er the land of the freeee

Barbara Cannon showed your reporter her souvenirs of the disaster: A life belt autographed by the crew and a severed human finger—

And the home of the brave

"I don't know," she said. "I feel sorta bad about this old finger."

Gave proof through the night that our flag was still there

SOS

The cold heavy fluid settled in a mountain village of slate houses where time stops—Blue twilight—Place Of The Silence Addicts—They move in and corner SOS and take it away in lead bottles and sit there on the nod in slate houses—On The Cool Blue or The Cold Grey—leave a wake of yapping ventriloquist dummies—They just sit there in cool blocks of blue silence and the earth's crust undulates under their weight of Heavy Time and Heavy Money—The Blue Heavy Metal People of Uranus—Heavy con men selling issues of fraudulent universe stock—It all goes back into SOS—[Solid Blue Silence.]

"Nobody can kick an SOS habit, kid—All the screams from The Pain Bank—from The Beginning you understand exploded deep in the tortured metal."

Junk poured through my screaming flesh—I got up and

danced The Junky Jig—I had my spoons—That's all I need—Into his spine falling some really great shit lately ("Shoot your way to peat bog") The cold heavy fluid settled—hydraulic beginning you understand—Exploded time stops in blue metal—Suburban galaxies on the nod—blue silence in the turnstile—village of slate houses—This foreign sun in bottles—

Martin came to Blue Junction in a heavy blue twilight where time stops—Slow hydraulic driver got out and moved away—Place of The Silent People—The Foreman showed him to The Bunk House—The men sat in blocks of cool blue silence at a long table and laid out photos in silent language of juxtaposition projecting the work—playing poker for position and advantage—

The work was hard and silent—There were irrigation canals and fish ponds with elaborate hydraulic locks and motors—The windmills and weather maps—(The Proprietor took photos of sky clouds and mountains every day moving arranging his weather maps in a vast flicker cylinder that turned with the wind on roof of The Main Building—Picture panels on walls of The Bunk House and Day Room changed with weather sky and mountain shadows in a silent blue twilight—The men took photos of each other and mixed picture composites shifting combos to wind and water sounds and frogs from the fish pools—(green pastures crisscrossed with black water and springs overhung with grass where Martin fished in the evening with Bradly who slept in the bunk next to his or in his bunk back and forth changing bodies in the blue silence—Tasks shifted with poker play and flesh trade—)

Blue—Flicker along the fish ponds—Blue shadows twilight—street—frogs and crickets—(crisscrossed my face)

The knife fell—The Clerk in the bunk next to his bled blue silence—Put on a clean shirt and Martin's pants—telling stories and exchanging smiles—dusty motors—The crop and fish talk muttering American dawn words—Sad rooming house—Picture wan light on suburban ponds and brown hair—Grey photo pools and springs over brass bed —Stale morning streets—sifting clouds and sky on my face —crisscrossed with city houses—

"Empty picture of a haunted ruin?" He lifted his hands sadly turned them out . . . "Some boy just wrote last good-bye across the sky . . . All the dream people of past time are saying good-bye forever, Mister" Late afternoon shadows against his back magic of all movies in remembered kid standing there face luminous by the attic window in a lost street of brick chimneys exploded star between us . . . You can look back along the slate shore to a white shirt flapping gunsmoke.

Short Count

The Heavy Metal Kid returned from a short blue holiday on Uranus and brought suit against practically everybody in The Biologic Courts—

"They are giving me a short count," he said in an interview with your reporter—"And I won't stand still for it—" Fade out

Corridors and patios and porticos of The Biologic Courts —Swarming with terminal life forms desperately seeking extension of canceled permissos and residence certificates —Brokers, fixers, runners, debarred lawyers, all claiming family connection with court officials—Professional half-brothers and second cousins twice removed—Petitioners and plaintiffs screaming through the halls—Holding up insect claws, animal and bird parts, all manner of diseases and deformities received "In the service" of distant fingers—Shrieking for compensations and attempting to corrupt or influence the judges in a thousand languages living and dead, in color flash and nerve talk,

catatonic dances and pantomimes illustrating their horrible
conditions which many have tattooed on their flesh to the
bone and silently picket the audience chamber—Others
carry photo-collage banners and TV screens flickering their
claims—Willy's attorneys served the necessary low pressure processes and The Controllers were sucked into
the audience chamber for the The First Hearing—Green
People in limestone calm—Remote green contempt for all
feelings and proclivities of the animal host they had invaded
with inexorable moves of Time-Virus-Birth-Death—With
their diseases and orgasm drugs and their sexless parasite
life forms—Heavy Metal People of Uranus wrapped in
cool blue mist of vaporized bank notes—And The Insect
People of Minraud with metal music—Cold insect brains
and their agents like white hot buzz saws sharpened in
the Ovens—The judge, many light years away from possibility of corruption, grey and calm with inflexible
authority reads the brief—He appears sometimes as a slim
young man in short sleeves then middle-aged and red-
faced sometimes very old like yellow ivory "My God what
a mess"—he said at last—"Quiet all of you—You all
understand I hope what is meant by biologic mediation—
This means that the mediating life forms must simul-
taneously lay aside all defenses and all weapons—it comes
to the same thing—and all connection with retrospective
controllers under space conditions merge into a single
being which may or may not be successful—" He glanced
at the brief—"It would seem that The Uranians represented
by the plaintiff Uranian Willy and The Green People
represented by Ali Juan Chapultepec are prepared to
mediate—Will these two uh personalities please stand
forward—Bueno—I expect that both of you would hesi-
tate if you could see—Fortunately you have not been uh
overbriefed—You must of course surrender all your
weapons and we will proceed with whatever remains—
Guards—Take them to the disinfection chambers and then

to The Biologic Laboratories"—He turned to The Controllers—"I hope they have been well prepared—I don't
need to tell you that—Of course this is only The First
Hearing—The results of mediation will be reviewed by a
higher court—"

Their horrible condition from a short blue holiday on
Uranus—Post everybody in The Biologic Courts: Willy's
attorney served "Count."—He said in an interview pushing
through and still for it—Fade out—Chambers—Green
People—remote green contempt forms fixers and runners
all claiming the animal hosts they had—(The Court Of
Professional Brothers and Moves Of Vegetable Centuries)
—The petitioners and plaintiffs their green sexless life
screaming through the halls remote mineral calm received
—in slate blue houses and catatonic dances illustrating
The Heavy Metal Kid returned—Many have tattooed in
diseases and brought suit against The Audience Chambers—

"They are giving me a short necessary process"—
Screaming crowds entered the corridors the audience and
the patios—The feeling and proclivities of connection with
officials invaded with inexorable limestone and cousins
twice removed—Virus and drugs plaintiff and defendant—
Heavy Metal People Of Uranus in a thousand languages
live robes that grow on them blue and hideous diseases—
The little high-fi junk note shrieking for compensation—
Spine frozen on the nod color flashes the heavy blue mist
of bank notes—The petitioners and plaintiffs screaming
through the halls wrapped in: "My God what a mess"—
Holding up insect claws remote with all understand I
hope what service—He appeared sometimes as whatever
remains—All understand I hope what proclivities of the
animal means that the mediating lie inexorable moves of
Time—

Twilight's Last Gleaming

The Gods of Time-Money-Junk gather in a heavy blue twilight drifting over bank floors to buy con force an extension of their canceled permits—They stand before The Man at The Typewriter—Calm and grey with inflexible authority he presents The Writ:

"Say only this should have been obvious from Her Fourth Grade Junk Class—Say only The Angel Profound Lord of Death—Say I have canceled your permissos through Time-Money-Junk of the earth—Not knowing what is and is not knowing I knew *not*. All your junk out in apomorphine—All your time and money out in word dust drifting smoke streets—Dream street of body dissolves in light . . ."

The Sick Junk God snatches The Writ: "Put him in The Ovens—Burn his writing"—He runs down a hospital corridor for The Control Switch—"He won't get far." A million police and partisans stand quivering electric dogs—antennae light guns drawn—

"You called The Fuzz—You lousy fink—"

"They are your police speaking your language—If you must speak you must answer in your language—"

"Stop—Alto—Halt—" Flashed through all I said a million silver bullets—The Junk God falls—Grey dust of broom swept out by an old junky in backward countries—

A heavy blue twilight drifting forward snatches The Writ—Time-Money-Junk gather to buy: "Put him in The Ovens—Burn his writing—"

"Say only The Angel Profound Lord of D—Runs down a hospital corridor—Your bodies I have written—Your death called the police—The Junk God sick from *"Stop—Alto—Halt—"* The Junk God falls in a heavy blue twilight drifting over the ready with drawn guns—Time-Money-Junk on all your languages—Yours—Must answer them—Your bodies—I have written your death hail of silver bullets—So we are now able to say *not*. Premature?? I think the auditor's mouth is stopped with his own—With her grey glance faded silver understanding out of date—Well I'd ask alterations but there really isn't time is there left by the ticket that exploded—Any case I have to move along—Little time so I'll say good night under the uh *circumstances*—Now the Spanish Flu would not be again at the window touching the wind in green neon— You understanding the room and she said: "Dear me what a long way down"—Meet Café is closed—if you wanted a cup of tea—burst of young you understand— so many and soo—The important thing is always courage to let go—in the dark—Once again he touched the window with his cool silver glance out into the cold spring air a colorless question drifted down corridors of that hospital—

"Thing Police keep all Board Room Reports"—And we are not allowed to proffer The Disaster Accounts—Wind hand caught in the door—Explosive Bio-Advance Men out of space to employ Electrician—In gasoline crack of history—Last of the gallant heroes—"I'm you on tracks Mr. Bradly Mr. Martin"—Couldn't reach flesh in his switch —And zero time to the sick tracks—A long time between suns I held the stale overcoat—Sliding between light and shadow—Muttering in the dogs of unfamiliar score— Cross the wounded galaxies we intersect—Poison of dead sun in your brain slowly fading—Migrants of ape in gasoline crack of history—Explosive bio advance out of space to neon—"I'm you, Wind Hand caught in the door—" Couldn't reach flesh—In sun I held the stale overcoat— Dead Hand stretching the throat—Last to proffer the disaster account on tracks—See Mr. Bradly Mr.—

And being blind may not refuse to hear: "Mr. Bradly Mr. Martin, disaster to my blood whom I created"—(The shallow water came in with the tide and the Swedish River of Gothenberg.)

THIS HORRIBLE CASE

ANGLE BOYS of the cosmos solicit from lavatories and broom closets of the Biologic Court Buildings charge out high on ammonia peddling fixes on any case from The Ovens Rap to a summons for biologic negligence—After buying a few short fixes in rigged courts, the pleaders defendants court officials and guilty bystanders learn to use a filter screen that scans out whole wave-lengths of ill-intentioned lunacy—This apparatus, sold in corridors and patios of the court buildings, enables any life form in need of legal advice to contact an accredited biologic counselor trained in the intricacies and apparent contradictions of biologic law—The classic case presented to first year students is The Oxygen Impasses: Life Form A arrives on alien planet from a crippled space craft—Life Form A breathes "oxygen"—There is no "oxygen" in the atmosphere of alien planet but by invading and occupying Life Form B native to alien planet they can convert the "oxygen" they need from the blood stream of Life Form B— The Occupying Life Form A directs all the behavior and energies of Host Life Form B into channels calculated to elicit the highest yield of oxygen—Health and interest of the host is disregarded—Development of the host to space stage is arrested since such development would deprive the invaders by necessity of their "oxygen" supply—For many years Life Form A remains invisible to Life Form B by a simple operation scanning out areas of perception where another life form can be seen—However an emergency a shocking emergency quite unlooked-for has arisen—Life Form B *sees* Life Form A—(Watching you have they thought debarred) and brings action in The Biologic Courts alleging unspeakable indignities, metal and physical cruelty, deterioration of mind body and soul over thousands of years, demanding summary removal of the alien parasite—To which Form A replies at The First Hearing: "It was a question of food supply—of absolute need— Everything followed from that: Iron claws of pain and pleasure squeezing a planet to keep the host in body prison working our 'oxygen' plants—Knowing that if he ever saw even for an instant who we are and what we are doing—(Switched our way is doomed in a few seconds)— And now he sees us planning to use the host as a diving suit back to our medium where of course Life Form B would be destroyed by alien conditions—Alternative posed by the aroused partisans fumbling closer and closer to the switch that could lock us out of Form B and cut our 'oxygen' lines—So what else could we do under the circumstances? The life form we invaded was totally alien and detestable to us—We do not have what they call 'emotions'—soft spots in the host marked for invasion and manipulation—"

The Oxygen Impasse is a basic statement in the algebra of absolute need—"Oxygen" interchangeable factor representing primary biologic need of a given life form—From this statement the students prepare briefs—sift cut and rearrange so they can view the case from varied angles and mediums:

The trial of The Nova Mob brought in emergency quite

unlooked-for: Broom arisen—sweeps Life Form B—*Sees*
fixes in The Biologic Courts—Deterioration of mind body
and soul buying a few short fixes in rigged Any Place—
Learns the years—the long—the many—such a place—
scans out whole lengths of alien parasite—and brings action
from unspeakable indignities and negligence demanding
summary biologic lawyers who never hustle a form—The
best criminal counselor was Uranian U—His clients from
heavy metal—Impression Thing followed from that Iron
Claws Brief—From one interview he got Sammy squeezing a planet in The Switch—The Green Octopus working
Vegetable Sentence—And now they have seen there is no
"oxygen" in the diving suit—Local life would be destroyed
by the "oxygen" they breathe—

"This pressure—Health cut our 'oxygen' lines—so
disregarded—"

"So *that* the circumstances?"

"Life of the host beyond 'THE' detestable to us—
Would deprive the invaders by soft spots in the host—"

With the material you have nature of absolute need and
The First Hearing in Biologic Court—

"Alleging you understand I must fight indignities and
cruelties and the natives are all mind body and soul demanding and I can't account for poison—(to which of
course I have never lost a client)—Specific facts and cases
a question of food supply not adequate—Owed from that
the two claws intimidate and corrupt—"

"Enables an arrested criminal of pleasure and pain to
squeeze counselor trained in the body-prison contradictions of biologic law—Diving suit of thousand years back
to our medium instead of The Reverse Switch—Alternative
Word Island—"

So where to first year students of Biologic Law Circumstances?—Life Form A was totally alien crippled space
craft—Do not have what they call "emotion's oxygen" in
the atmosphere—

119

A student who represents Life Form A must anticipate questions of the Biologic Prosecutor:—

"How did the space craft 'happen' to be crippled in such convenient proximity?—Was not the purpose of the expedition to find 'oxygen' and extract it by any means?—During many years of occupancy was any effort towards biologic reconversion made by Life Form A prior to intervention of The Biologic Police?—Was not Life Form A conspiring to cut off the 'oxygen' of Life Form B as soon as their 'travel arrangements' were completed? Did they not in fact plan to liquidate Life Form B by cutting off 'emotion's oxygen' the charge on which human and other mammalian life forms run?—(Doctor W. Reich has suggested that human life is activated by units he calls 'orgones' which form a belt around the planet)—Life Form A obviously conspired to blockade the orgone belt and leave Form B to suffocate in a soulless vacuum at the high surface temperatures that obtain on Life Form A's planet of origin: 600 Degrees Fahrenheit—"

In short the plea of need offered by Life Form A is inadequate—To prepare a case would be necessary to investigate the original conditions and biologic history of Life Form A on location—A Biologic Counselor must know his client and be "trained in the body-prison contradictions of biologic law"—It will not be easy for Life Form A to find a counselor willing to handle "this horrible case—"

Brief for the First Hearing

Biologic Counselors must be writers that is only writers can qualify since the function of a counselor is to *create* facts that will tend to open biologic potentials for his client —One of the great early counselors was Franz Kafka and his briefs are still standard—The student first writes his own brief then folds his pages down the middle and lays it on pages of Kafka relevant to the case in hand—(It is not always easy to say what is and is not relevant)—To indicate the method here is tentative brief for The First Hearing in Biologic Court:—A preparation derived from one page of Kafka passed through the student's brief and the original statement back and forth until a statement of biologic position emerges—From this original statement the student must now expand his case—

QUOTE FROM *The Trial*—FRANZ KAFKA

"I fancy," said the man who was stylishly dressed, "that the gentleman's faintness is due to the atmosphere here— You see it's only here that this gentleman feels upset, not in other places—" Accustomed as they were to the office air felt ill in the relatively fresh air that came up from the stairway—They could scarcely answer him and the girl might have fallen if K had not shut the door with the utmost haste—He had already, so he would relate, won many similar cases either outright or partially—That was very important for the first impression made by the defense frequently determined the whole course of subsequent proceedings—Especially when a case they had conducted was suddenly taken out of their hands—That was beyond all doubt the worst thing that could happen to an advocate—Not that a client ever dismissed an advocate from the case—For how could he keep going by himself once he had pulled in someone to help him?— But it did sometimes happen that a case took a turn where the advocate could no longer follow it—The case and the accused and everything was simply withdrawn from the advocate—Then even the best connection with officials could no longer achieve any result—For even they knew nothing—The case had simply reached the stage where further assistance was ruled out—It had vanished into remote inaccessible courts where even the accused was beyond the reach of an advocate—The advocate's room was in the very top attic so that if you stumbled through the hole your leg hung down into the lower attic in the very corridor where the clients had to wait—

Brief for First Hearing //
Case of Life Form A

They sometimes mutate to breathe *"here"*—The gentleman *is* Biologic Court Building *"here"*—You see it's only *"here"* fixes any case from The Ovens—Not in other places —after buying the relatively fresh air—Life Form A arrives on worst thing that could happen to a space craft— Life Form A breathes from the atmosphere of alien planet—Form A directs all behavior withdrawn from the advocate into channels calculated to no longer achieve health and interest of the host—The case had simply reached to space stage—Assistance was ruled out—Even the accused was beyond years—Life Form A's room was in the very top—

"I fancy," said the man who was on alien planet, "that crippled faintness is due to the 'oxygen'—There is no 'oxygen' this gentleman feels but by invading and occupying 'the office air' they can convert the 'oxygen' up from the stairway of Life Form B."

The first impression made determines whole course of subsequent "oxygen" supply—A shocking emergency case —For how could he keep Form A??—Sees someone to help him but it debarred action in turn—Could scarcely answer the people of Minraud—Brain directs all movement—Use a filter screen that scans the door with intentioned lunacy—Won many similar cases operating through telepathic misdirection—There has been dismissed an advocate from Minraud—Pulled in and replaced— Worst thing that could happen to present heads—Sometimes happened that a case took total weapons—The principal no longer follow it—The case had simply reached molten core of a planet where assistance was ruled out—

"I fancy," said the man, "that this gentleman feels white hot blue skies—Haste he had already so?"

Even so there is a devious underground either outright or partial misdirection—The office air are heads in bottles —Beyond all doubt intend to outthink and replace the advocate—A client revolution—For how could he keep fallen heads to help him?—Metal shimmering heat from the stage where further assistance melts at noon into remote inaccessible courts—

"Word falling—Photo falling stylishly dressed—The gentleman's insane orders and counter orders 'here'— You see it's only 'here'—Accustomed D.C. felt ill in the relatively fresh air, what?—British could scarcely answer him—Shut the door with the utmost haste—"

"Mindless idiot you have won many similar cases—"

Electric defense frequently determined the whole civilization and proceedings—Especially when a case fear desperate position and advantage suddenly taken out of their hands—The case had simply reached incredible life forms—Even the accused was beyond altered pressure— The very top operation—The client of mucus and urine said the man was an alien—Unusual mucus coughing enemy "oxygen" up from the stairway—Speed up movie made such forms by overwhelming gravity supply—Flesh frozen to supply a shocking emergency case—Amino acid directs all movement—won code on Grey Veil—To be read telepathic misdirection—"Office air" they can convert in dirty pictures of Life Form B—liquidate enemy on London Space Stage—Tenuous air debarred action of yesterday—Coughing enemy pulled in and replaced—

"The gentleman in body prison working our 'here'— You see it's only 'here' he ever saw even for an instant— Not in other places—Switched our way is doomed in the relatively fresh air—That's us—Planning to use the host could scarcely answer him—Of course Life Form B with the utmost haste would shut the door that was very important for our 'oxygen' lines—So what else?—Defense frequently determined the life form we invaded—"

Especially when a case marked for invasion and manipulation suddenly taken out of their hands—Dismissed an advocate from Biologic Need once he had you pulled in to prepare briefs—The trial of The Nova Mob withdrawn from the advocate—The case had simply reached rigged any place—Pain and pleasure to squeeze the "office air" felt contradictions of biologic stairway—Crippled in such convenient advocate—For how could he keep means during many years of someone to help him?—

"I fancy faintness is due to the atmosphere offered by Life Form A is inadequate—That this gentleman feels necessary to investigate the original 'office air' story of Life Form A on location—A came up from the stairway —He had already counselor willing to handle 'this horrible case' either outright or partially—You see it's only *'here'* fixes nature of absolute need—A question of food supply not alien planet—Form A direct claws intimidate and corrupt advocate into channels calculated to squeeze host— Assistance back to our medium—"

Life Form A's room was on Ward Island—Crippled in such convenient Life Form B—Minraud an intricate door to cut off "oxygen" of life—Similar case operating through arrangements that could liquidate Life Form B by cutting off advocate from Minraud—

"Life Form A was totally alien," said the man who was an alien—

"Have what they call 'emotion' due to the 'oxygen.'"

"Was not the purpose supply Life Form A prior to intervention directing all movement?"

"Pleader a diving suit back to our medium—Scarcely answer him—Be destroyed by alien conditions—Ally detestable to us—For how could he keep Form A seen parasite?"

The best criminal counselor was similar case operating through metal—Impression followed to present interview —He got Sammy advocate from Minraud—Pulled in and replaced history of Life Form A on location—

Clearly this is a difficult case to defend particularly considering avowed intention of the accused to use the counselor as a diving suit back to their medium where counselor would be destroyed by alien conditions—There is however one phrase in the brief on which a defense can be constructed—"They sometimes mutate to breathe here" —That is if a successful mutation of Life Form A can be called in as witness—Clearly the whole defense must be based on possibility of mutation and the less said about "absolute biologic need" to maintain a detrimental parasitic existence at the total expense of Form B the better chance of a compromise verdict suspended pending mutation proceedings—

Two Tape Recorder Mutations

"I fancy," said the man, "this gentleman feels totally stupid and greedy Venus Power—Tentacles write out message from stairway of slime—"

"That's us—Strictly from 'Sogginess Is Good For You' —Planning no bones but an elementary nervous system— Scarcely answer him—"

"The case simply at terminal bring down point— Desperate servants suddenly taken out of their hands— Insane orders and counter orders on the horizon—And I playing psychic chess determined the whole civilization and personal habits—"

"Iron claws of pain and pleasure with two speeds— with each recorder in body prison working our 'here' on extension leads—Even for an instant not in operation the host recorder saw the loudspeakers—Way is doomed in relatively soundproof 'room'—Would shift door led to the array—Many recorders important for our oxygen lines—Each to use host connected to its respective recorder layout—For example with nine recorders determined the life form we invaded by three square—Each recorder marked for invasion recording—You see it's only 'here' fixes nature of need set to run for as long as required— 'Indignities' and 'cruelties' are playing back while other record—'Intimidate' and 'corrupt' speed and volume variation—Squeeze host back into system—Any number of tape recorders banked together for ease of operation switch in other places—Our mikes are laid out preferably in 'fresh air'—That's us—Planning speaker and mike connected to host—Scarcely answer him—Of course static and moving are possible—Very simplest array would be three lines— Two speeds can be playing especially when a 'case' has four possible states—Fast manipulation suddenly taken out of slow playback—The actual advocate from biologic need in many ways—

"a-Simple hand switching advocate

"b-Random choice fixed interval biologic stairway— The whole thing is switched on either outright or partially —at any given time recorders fix nature of absolute need— Thus sound played back by any 'cruelties' answer him either unchanged or subject to alien planet—

"c-Sequential choice i.e. flesh frozen to amino acid determines the next state according to"—That is a "book"—

Form A directs sound channels—Continuous operation in such convenient Life Form B—Final switching off of tape cuts "oxygen" Life Form B by cutting off machine will produce cut-up of human form determined by the switching chosen—Totally alien "music" need not survive in any "emotion" due to the "oxygen" rendered down to a form of music—Intervention directing all movement what will be the end product?—Reciprocation detestable to us for how could we become part of the array?—Could this metal impression follow to present language learning? —Talking and listening machine led in and replaced—

Life Form A as follows was an alien—The operator selects the most "oxygen" appropriate material continuous diving suit back to our medium—Ally information at the verbal level—Could he keep Form A seen parasitic?—Or could end be achieved by present interview?—Array treated as a whole replaced history of life? Word falling photo falling tapes being blank—Insane orders and counter orders of machine "music"—The Police Machine will produce a cut-up of it determined by the switching chosen —Could this alien mucus cough language learn? Accused was beyond altered sound formations—Alien Mucus Machine runs by feeding in overwhelming gravity—Code on Grey Veil parallel the spread of "dirty pictures"—Reverse instruction raises question how many convert in "dirty pictures" before London Space Stage—Tenuous simple repetition to one machine only—Coughing enemy pulled in whole could be used as a model for behavior—Screams laughter shouts raw material—Voice fading into advocate:

"Clearly the whole defense must be experiments with two tape recorder mutations."

PAY COLOR

"THE SUBLIMINAL KID" moved in and took over bars cafés and juke boxes of the world cities and installed radio transmitters and microphones in each bar so that the music and talk of any bar could be heard in all his bars and he had tape recorders in each bar that played and recorded at arbitrary intervals and his agents moved back and forth with portable tape recorders and brought back street sound and talk and music and poured it into his recorder array so he set waves and eddies and tornadoes of sound down all your streets and by the river of all language—Word dust drifted streets of broken music car horns and air hammers—The Word broken pounded twisted exploded in smoke—

Word Falling ///

He set up screens on the walls of his bars opposite mirrors and took and projected at arbitrary intervals shifted from one bar to the other mixing Western Gangster films of all time and places with word and image of the people in his cafés and on the streets his agents with movie camera and telescope lens poured images of the city back into his projector and camera array and nobody knew whether he was in a Western movie in Hongkong or The Aztec Empire in Ancient Rome or Suburban America whether he was a bandit a commuter or a chariot driver whether he was firing a "real" gun or watching a gangster movie and the city moved in swirls and eddies and tornadoes of image explosive bio-advance out of space to neon—

Photo Falling ///

"The Subliminal Kid" moved in seas of disembodied sound—He then spaced here and there and instaff opposite mirrors and took movies each bar so that the music and talk is at arbitrary intervals and shifted bars—And he also had recorder in tracks and moving film mixing arbitrary intervals and agents moving with the word and image of tape recorders—So he set up waves and his agents with movie swirled through all the streets of image and brought back street in music from the city and poured Aztec Empire and Ancient Rome—Commuter or Chariot Driver could not control their word dust drifted from outer space—Air hammers word and image explosive bio-advance—A million drifting screens on the walls of his city projected mixing sound of any bar could be heard in all Westerns and film of all times played and recorded at the people back and forth with portable cameras and telescope lenses poured eddies and tornadoes of sound and camera array until soon city where he moved everywhere a Western movie in Hongkong or the Aztec sound talk suburban America and all accents and language mixed and fused and people shifted language and accent in mid-sentence Aztec priest and spilled it man woman or beast in all language—So that People-City moved in swirls and no one knew what he was going out of space to neon streets—

"Nothing Is True—Everything Is Permitted—" Last *Words Hassan I Sabbah*

The Kid stirred in sex films and The People-City pulsed in a vast orgasm and no one knew what was film and what was not and performed all kinda sex acts on every street corner—

He took film of sunsets and cloud and sky water and tree film and projected color in vast reflector screens concentrating blue sky red sun green grass and the city dissolved in light and people walked through each other—There was only color and music and silence where the words of Hassan i Sabbah had passed—

"Boards Syndicates Governments of the earth *Pay*— Pay back the *Color* you stole—

"Pay Red—Pay back the red you stole for your lying flags and your Coca-Cola signs—Pay that red back to penis and blood and sun—

"Pay Blue—Pay back the blue you stole and bottled and doled out in eye droppers of junk—Pay back the blue you stole for your police uniforms—Pay that blue back to sea and sky and eyes of the earth—

"Pay Green—Pay back the green you stole for your money—And you, Dead Hand Stretching The Vegetable People, pay back the green you stole for your Green Deal to sell out peoples of the earth and board the first life boat in drag—Pay that green back to flowers and jungle river and sky—

"Boards Syndicates Governments of the earth pay back your stolen colors—*Pay Color* back to Hassan i Sabbah—"

Pay Off the Marks?

Amusement park to the sky—The concessioners gathered in a low pressure camouflage pocket—

131

"I tell you Doc the marks are out there pawing the
ground,

" 'What's this Green Deal?'

" 'What's this Sky Switch?'

" 'What's this Reality Con?'

" 'Man, we been short-timed?'

" 'Are you a Good Gook?'

" 'A good Nigger?'

" 'A Good Human Animal?'

"They'll take the place apart—I've seen it before—
like a silver flash—And The Law is moving in—Not
locals—This is Nova Heat—I tell we got to give and
fast—Flicker, The Movies, Biologic Merging Tanks, The
lot—Well, Doc?"

"It goes against my deepest instincts to pay off the
marks—But under the uh circumstances—caught as we
are between an aroused and not in all respects reasonable
citizenry and the antibiotic handcuffs—"

The Amusement Gardens cover a continent—There
are areas of canals and lagoons where giant gold fish
and salamanders with purple fungoid gills stir in clear
black water and gondolas piloted by translucent green
fish boys—Under vast revolving flicker lamps along the
canals spill The Biologic Merging Tanks sense withdrawal
capsules light and soundproof water at blood temperature
pulsing in and out where two life forms slip in and merge
to a composite being often with deplorable results slated for
Biologic Skid Row on the outskirts: (Sewage delta and
rubbish heaps—terminal addicts of SOS muttering down to
water worms and floating vegetables—Paralyzed Orgasm
Addicts eaten alive by crab men with white hot eyes or
languidly tortured in charades by The Green Boys of young
crystal cruelty)

Vast communal immersion tanks melt whole peoples
into one concentrate—It's more democratic that way you
see?—Biologic Representation—Cast your vote into the

tanks—Here where flesh circulates in a neon haze and identity tags are guarded by electric dogs sniffing quivering excuse for being—The assassins wait broken into scanning patterns of legs smile and drink—Unaware of The Vagrant Ball Player pant smell running in liquid typewriter—

Streets of mirror and glass and metal under flickering cylinders of colored neon—Projector towers sweep the city with color writing of The Painter—Cool blue streets between walls of iron polka-dotted with lenses projecting The Blue Tattoo open into a sea of Blue Concentrate lit by pulsing flickering blue globes—Mountain villages under the blue twilight—Drifting cool blue music of all time and place to the brass drums—

Street of The Light Dancers who dance with color writing projected on their bodies in spotlight layers peel off red yellow blue in dazzling strip acts, translucent tentative beings flashing through neon hula hoops—stand naked and explode in white fade out in grey—vaporize in blue twilight—

Who did not know the name of his vast continent?—There were areas left at his electric dogs—Purple fungoid gills stirred in being—His notebooks running flicker screens along the canals—

"Who him?—Listen don't let him out here."

Two life forms entered the cracked earth to escape terrible dry heat of The Insect People—The assassins wait legs by water cruel idiot smiles play a funeral symphony—For being he was caught in the zoo—Cages snarling and coming on already—The Vagrant passed down dusty Arab street muttering: "Where is he now?" —Listening sifting towers swept the city—American dawn words falling on my face—Cool Sick room with rose wallpaper—"Mr. Bradly Mr. Martin" put on a clean shirt and walked out—stars and pool halls and stale rooming house—this foreign sun in your brain—visit of memories

and wan light—silent suburban poker—worn pants—
scratching shower room and brown hair—grey photo—on
a brass bed—stale flesh exploded film in basement toilets—
boys jack off from—this drifting cobweb of memories—
in the wind of morning—furtive and sad felt the lock
click—

He walked through—Summer dust—stirring St. Louis
schoolrooms—a brass bed—Cigarette smoke—urine as in
the sun—Soccer scores and KiKi when I woke up—Such
wisdom in gusts—empty spaces—Fjords and Chimborazi
—brief moments I could describe to the barrier—Pursuits
of future life where boy's dawn question is far away—
What's St. Louis or any conveyor distance? St. Louis on
this brass bed? Comte Wladmir Sollohub Rashid Ali
Khan B Bremond d'Ars Marquis de Migre Principle di
Castelcicale Gentilhomo di Palazzo you're a long way
from St. Louis . . . Let me tell you about a score of years'
dust on the window that afternoon I watched the torn sky
bend with the wind . . . *white white white as far as the eye
can see ahead a blinding flash of white* . . . (The cabin
reeks of exploded star). . . . Broken sky through my
nostrils—Dead bare knee against the greasy dust—Faded
photo drifting down across pubic hair, thighs, rose wallpaper into the streets of Pasto—The urinals and the
bicycle races here in this boy were gone when I woke up—
Whiffs of my Spain down the long empty noon—Brief
moments I could describe—The great wind revolving lips
and pants in countries of the world—Last soldier's fading
—Violence is shut off Mr. Bradly Mr.—I am dying in a
room far away—last—Sad look—Mr. Of The Account,
I am dying—In other flesh now Such dying—Remember
hints as we shifted windows the visiting moon air like
death in your throat?—The great wind revolving lip
smoke, fading photo and distance—Whispers of junk,
flute walks, shirt flapping—Bicycle races here at noon—
boy thighs—Sad—Lost dog—He had come a long way

for something not exchanged . . . sad shrinking face . . .
He died during the night. . . .

Smorbrot

Operation Sense Withdrawal* is carried out in silent
lightless immersion tanks filled with a medium of salt
bouillon at temperature and density of the human body
—Cadets enter the tank naked and free floating a few
inches apart—permutate on slow currents—soon lose
the outlines of body in shifting contact with phantom limbs
—Loss of outline associated with pleasant sensations—
frequently orgasms occur—
K9 took off his clothes in a metal-lined cubicle with a
Chinese youth—Naked he felt vertigo and a tightening
of stomach muscles as they let themselves down into the
tank and floated now a few inches apart warm liquid
swirling through legs and genitals touching—His hands
and feet lost outline—There was sudden sharp spasm in
his throat and a taste of blood—The words dissolved—
His body twisted in liquid fish spasms and emptied through

* The most successful method of sense withdrawal is the
immersion tank where the subject floats in water at blood
temperature sound and light withdrawn—loss of body outline, awareness and location of the limbs occurs quickly, giving rise to panic in many American subjects—Subjects frequently report feeling that another body is floating half in
and half out of the body in the first part—Experiments in
sense withdrawal using the immersion tanks have been performed by Doctor Lilly in Florida—There is another experimental station in Oklahoma—So after fifteen minutes in the
tank these marines scream they are losing outlines and have
to be removed—I say put two marines in the tank and see
who comes out—Science—Pure science—So put a marine
and his girl friend in the tank and see who or what
emerges—

his spurting penis—feeling other spasms shiver through the tank—He got out and dresses with a boy from The Alameda—Back in flesh—street boy words in his throat— Kerosene light on a Mexican about twenty felt his pants slide down his stomach his crotch unbuttoned sighed and moved his ass off—He was naked now in lamp—Mexican rolled marijuana cigarette—naked body of the other next to his turning him over on his stomach—his crotch unbuttoned wind and water sounds—sighed and moved his ass in shadow pools on rose wallpaper—brass bed stale against him—Felt naked body of the other explode in his spine— Room changed with flesh—Felt his pants slide—The cadet's ass was naked now—A few inches apart in the tank the Mexican—His lips felt propositions—A few inches apart K9 moved his ass in scratching shower—Wave of pleasure through his stomach—He was floating moving in food—City of Chili Houses exploded in muscles and the words went in—There in his throat—Kerosene light on with street boy—Outskirts of The City—First spurts of his crotch—

The naked cadets entered a warehouse of metal-lined cubicles—stood a few inches apart laughing and talking on many levels—Blue light played over their bodies*—

* Reference to the orgone accumulators of Doctor Wilhelm Reich—Doctor Reich claims that the basic charge of life is this blue orgone-like electrical charge—Orgones form a sphere around the earth and charge the human machine— He discovered that orgones pass readily through iron but are stopped and absorbed by organic matter—So he constructed metal-lined cubicles with layers of organic material behind the metal—Subjects sit in the cubicles lined with iron and accumulate orgones according to the law of increased returns on which life functions—The orgones produce a prickling sensation frequently associated with erotic stimulation and spontaneous orgasm—Reich insists that orgasm is an electrical discharge—He has attached electrodes to the appropriate connections and charted the orgasm—In con-

Projectors flashed the color writing of Hassan i Sabbah on bodies and metal walls—Opened into amusement gardens —Sex Equilibrists perform on tightropes and balancing chairs—Trapeze acts ejaculate in the air—The Sodomite Tumblers doing cartwheels and whirling dances stuck together like dogs—Boys masturbate from scenic railways —Flower floats in the lagoons and canals—Sex cubicles where the acts performed to music project on the tent ceiling a sky of rhythmic copulation—Vast flicker cylinders and projectors sweep the gardens writing explosive bio-advance to neon—Areas of sandwich booths blue movie parlors and transient hotels under ferris wheels and scenic railways—soft water sounds and frogs from the canals— K9 stood opposite a boy from Norway felt the prickling blue light on his genitals filling with blood touched the other tip and a warm shock went down his spine and he came in spasms of light—Silver writing burst in his brain and went out with a smell of burning metal in empty intersections where boys on roller skates turn slow circles and weeds grow through cracked pavement—

Mexican rolled cigarette the soft blue light deep in his lungs—Mexican hands touching felt his pants slide down in soundless explosion of the throat and a taste of blood— His body twisted—Sleeps naked now—wind and water sounds—Outskirts of the city—shadow areas of sandwich booths and transient hotels under scenic railways—

sequence of these experiments he was of course expelled from various countries before he took refuge in America and died in a federal penitentiary for suggesting the orgone accumulator in treating cancer—It has occurred to this investigator that orgone energy can be concentrated to disperse the miasma of idiotic prurience and anxiety that blocks any scientific investigation of sexual phenomenon— Preliminary experiments indicate that certain painting— like Brion Gysin's—when projected on a subject produced some of the effects observed in orgone accumulators—

We drank the beer and ate the smorbrot—I dropped half a sandwich in my lap and she wiped the butter off with a napkin laughing as the cloth bulged under her fingers my back against a tree the sun on my crotch tingling filling with blood she opened my belt and: "Raise up, darling," pulled my pants down to the knee—
We ate the smorbrot with hot chocolate from the thermos bottle and I spilled a cup of chocolate in my lap and jumped up and she wiped the chocolate off with a paper napkin and I dodged away laughing as the cloth bulged under her fingers and she followed me with the napkin and opened my belt—I felt my pants slide down and the sun on my naked crotch tingling and filling with blood—We did it half undressed—When I came there was silver light popped in my eyes like a flash bulb and looking over her shoulder I saw little green men in the trees swinging from branch to branch turning cartwheels in the air—And sex acts by naked acrobats on tightropes and balancing poles—Jissom drifting cobwebs through clear green light—Washed in the stream and pulled up my pants—We rode back to Copenhagen on my motor scooter —I left her in front of her flat block and arranged a meeting for Sunday—As she walked away I could see the grass stains on the back of her dress—That night I was blank and went back to bar in Neuerhaven where I can usually find a tourist to buy drinks—and sat down at a table with a boy about my age—I noticed he had a very small narrow head tapering from his neck which was thick and smooth and something strange about his eyes—The iris was shiny black like broken coal with pinpoint green pupils—He turned and looks straight at me and I got a feeling like scenic railways in the stomach—Then he ordered two beers—"I see that you are blank," he said— The beers came—"I work with the circus," he said— balancing his chair—"Like this on wires—never with net

—In South America I did it over a gorge of a thousand meters in depth."

Balancing he drank the Tuborg—"There are not many who can see us—Come and I will show you our real acts."

We took a cab to the outskirts of the city—There was a warm electric wind blowing through the car that seemed to leave the ground—We came to what looked like a ruined carnival by a lake—In a tent lit by flickering blue globes I met more boys with the same narrow head and reversed eyes—They passed around a little pipe and I smoked and felt green tingling in my crotch and lips—A Negro drummer began pounding his drum with sticks—The boys got up laughing and passing the pipe and talking in a language like bird calls and took off their clothes—They climbed a ladder to the high wire and walked back and forth like cats—A magic lantern projected color writing on their bodies that looked like Japanese tattooing—They all got erections and arching past each other on the wire genitals touched in a shower of blue sparks—One boy balanced a steel chair on the wire and ejaculated in a crescendo of drum beats and flickering rainbow colors—jissom turning slow cartwheels dissolved in yellow light—Another boy with earphones crackling radio static and blue sparks playing around his yellow hair did a Messer-schmidt number—the chair rocking in space—tracer bullets of jissom streaking cross interstellar void—(Naked boys on roller skates turn slow circles at the intersection of ruined suburbs—falling through a maze of penny arcades—spattered the cracked concrete weeds and dog excrement—) The boys came down from the wire and one of them flicked my jacket—I took off my clothes and practiced balancing naked in a chair—The balance point was an electrical field holding him out of gravity—The charge built up in his genitals and he came in a wet dream the

139

chair fluid and part of his body—That night made sex
with the boy I met in Neuerhaven for the first time with
each other in space—Sure calm of wire acts balanced on
ozone—blue electric spasms—Smell of burning metal in
the penny arcade I got a hard on looking at the peep show
and Hans laughed pointing to my fly: "Let's make the
roller coaster," he said—The cashier took our money with
calm neutral glance—A young Italian clicked us out—
We were the only riders and as soon as the car started we
slipped off our shorts—We came together in the first dip
as the car started up the other side throwing blood into our
genitals tight and precise as motor parts—open shirts
flapping over the midway—Silver light popped in my
head and went out in blue silence—Smell of ozone—You
see sex is an electrical charge that can be turned on and
off if you know the electromagnetic switchboard—Sex is
an electrical flesh trade—It is usually turned on by water
sounds—Now take your sex words on rose wallpaper
brass bed—Explode in red brown green from colors to
the act on the association line—Naked charge can explode
sex words to color's rectal brown green ass language—
The sex charge is usually controlled by sex words forming
an electromagnetic pattern—This pattern can be shifted
by substituting other factors for words—Take a simple sex
word like "masturbate"—"jack off"—Substitute color for
the words like: "jack"—red "off"—white—red—white—
Flash from words to color on the association screen—
Associate silently from colors to the act—Substitute other
factors for the words—Arab drum music—Musty smell
of erections in outhouses—Feel of orgasm—Color-music-
smell-feel to the million sex acts all time place—Boys
red-white from ferris wheel, scenic railways, bridges,
whistling bicycles, tree houses careening freight cars train
whistles drifting jissom in winds of Panhandle—shivering
through young bodies under boarding house covers rubbly
outskirts of South American city ragged pants dropped to

cracked bleeding feet black dust blowing through legs and genitals—Pensive lemur smell of erection—cool basement toilets in St. Louis—Summer afternoon on car seats to the thin brown knee—Bleak public school flesh naked for the physical the boy with epilepsy felt The Dream in his head struggling for control locker room smells on his stomach—He was in The Room with many suitcases all open and drawers full of things that had to be packed and only a few minutes to catch the boat whistling in the harbor and more and more drawers and the suitcases won't close arithmetical disorder and the wet dream tension in his crotch—The other boys laughing and pointing in the distance now as he got out of control silver light popped in his eyes and he fell with a sharp metal cry—through legs and genitals felt his pants slide—shivering outskirts of the city—wind of morning in a place full of dust—Naked for a physical orgasms occur—tightening stomach muscles— scenic railways exploded in his crotch—Legs and genitals lost outline careening through dream flesh—smell of the mud flats—warm spurts to sluggish stream water from the tree house—a few inches apart laughing in the sunlight jissom cartwheels in the clear air of masturbating afternoons—pulled up my pants—Explosion of the throat from color to the act jumped up laughing in the transient hotels —careening area of sandwich booths—Silver writing burst in moonlight through a Mexican about twenty shifting his crotch sighed and moved naked now a few inches in his hand—pleasure tingling through cracked bleeding feet— With phantom limbs his cock got hard sensations on roller skates—slow intersection of weeds and concrete— Penny arcades spattered light on a Mexican about twenty— Wet dreams of flight sighed in lamp—Flash from word to color sex acts all time place exploded in muscles drifting sheets of male flesh—Boys on wind of morning—first spurts unbuttoned my pants—Area of sandwich booths and intolerable scenic railways he came wet dream way—(In

the tree house black ants got into our clothes pulling off
shirts and pants and brushing the ants off each other he
kept brushing my crotch—"there's an ant there" and
jacked me off into the stream of masturbating afternoons)
—Hans laughed pointing to my shorts—Pants to the ankle
we were the only riders—Wheee came together in the first
dip open shorts flapping genitals—Wind of morning
through flesh—Outskirts of the city—

Its Accounts

Now hazard flakes fall—A huge wave rolled treatment
"pay back the red you stole"—Farewell for Alexander—
Fading out in Ewyork, Onolulu, Aris, Ome, Oston—Sub
editor melted into air—I Sekuin hardly breathe—Dreams
are made of might be just what I am look: Prerecorded
warning in a woman's voice—Scio is pulling a figure out
of logos—A huge wave bowled a married couple off what
you could have—Would you permit that person in Ewyork,
Onolulu, Aris, Ome, Oston?—One assumes a "beingness"
where past crimes highlighted the direction of a "havingness"—He boasted of a long string of other identities—She
gave no indication of fundamental agreement—We returned to war—Process pre-clear in absurd position for
conditions—Scio is like pulling a figure out of The Homicide Act—Logos got Sheraton Call and spent the weekend
with a bargain—Venus Vigar choked to passionate weak-
ness—The great wind identity failed—So did art loving
Miss West—Every part of your dust yesterday along the
High Street Air—The flakes fall that were his cruelest
lawyer: show you fear on walls and windows treatment—
Farewell trouble for Alexander—Pay back the red you
stole living or dead from the sky—Hurry up please its
accounts—Empty thing police they fading out—Dusk
through narrow streets, toilet paper, and there is no light

in the window—April wind revolving illness of dead sun—
Woman with red hair is a handful of dust—Departed have
left used avenue—Many years ago that youngster—It was
agony to breathe in number two intake—Dreams of the
dead—Prerecorded warning—Remember I was carbon
dioxide—It is impossible to estimate the years in novitiate
postulating Sheraton Carlton Call—Loose an arrow—
Thud—Thing Police fading out in Ewyork, Onolulu, Aris,
Ome, Oston—See where he struck—Oh no discounts and
compensations—Stop tinkering with what you could have
—Must go in time—Stop tinkering with recompense—
You'll know me in dark mutinous mirrors of the world—
Yesterday along high street massive treatment: "Pay back
the red you stole"—A shame to part with it?? Try various
farewell trouble?? Near curtains for them and trouble
shuffled out of the die—Along high street account reaching
to my chest—Pay back the red you stole happened—
Effects Boys said farewell to Alexander Bargain—"What
are we going to do? Thing police they fading out—Sub
editor melted into air—So I had to do Two Of A Kind
on toilet paper—Obvious sooner that air strip."

"It was agony to breathe—What might be called the
worried in number two intake—Barry going to do?—
Partisans of all nations learn all about it—Red Hair we
were getting to use on anyone—Pit too—Going to get
out of it?"

A colorless question drifted down corridors of that
hospital—"I Sekuin—Tell me what you would permit to
remain?"

Simple as a Hiccup

Mr. Martin, hear us through something as simple as a
hiccup tinkering with the disaster accounts—All Board
Room Reports are classified as narcotic drugs—Morphine

is actually "Mr. Martin," his air line the addict—I have said the basic techniques: every reason to believe the officers dictate in detail with a precise repetition of stimuli place of years—Techniques of nova reports are stimuli between enemies—Dimethyltryptamine pain bank from "disagreeable symptoms"—Overdose by precise repetition can be nightmare experience owing to pain headphones send nova spirit from Hiroshima and Nagasaki—"Mr. Martin," hear us through mushroom clouds—Start tinkering with disaster brains and twisting all board room reports —Their pain line is the addict—Pain bank from the torture chambers—Every reason to believe the officers torn into insect fragments by precise repetition of years—Tortured metal pain spirit Uranian born of nova conditions send those blasts—Great wind revolving the nova spirit in image flakes—Every part of your translucent burning fire head shut off, Mr. Bradly, in the blue sky writing of Hassan i Sabbah—That hospital melted in Grey Room—Writing of Hassan i Sabbah postulating you were all smoke drifting from something as simple as a hiccup—I have said the basic techniques of the world and mutilated officers dictate in detail with iron claws of the chessmen place of years— Hassan i Sabbah through all disaster accounts—Last door of nova and all the torture expanding drugs—Pressure groups teach mechanisms involved—Disaster of nova pulsed need dictates use of throat bones—I Sabbah walk in the recordings write dripping faucet and five flashes per second—The rhythmic turrets destroy enemy installations —Cortex winds overflowing into mutinous areas hearing color seeing "Mr. Bradly Mr. Martin"—Just time—Just time—I quote from Anxiety And Its Treatment in Grey Room—Apomorphine as a hiccup—Hassan i Sabbah through apomorphine acts on the hypothalamus and regulates blood serum of the world and mutilated officers— Melted a categorical "no mercy for this enemy" as dust and smoke—

There's a Lot Ended

New York, Saturday March 17, Present Time—For many he accidentally blew open present food in The Homicide Act—Anyway after that all the top England spend the weekend with a bargain—Intend to settle price —I had work in Melbourne before doing sessions— Australia in the gates—Dogs must be carried—Reluctant to put up any more Amplex—Go man go—There's a lot ended—Flashes The Maharani of Check Moth—The clean queen walks serenely down dollars—Don't listen to Hassan i Sabbah—We want Watney's Woodbines and all pleasures of the body—Stand clear of The Garden of Delights—And love slop is a Bristol—Bring together state of news— Inquire on hospital—At the Ovens Great Gold Cup— Revived peat victory hopes of Fortria—Premature Golden sands in Sheila's cottage?—You want the name of Hassan i Sabbah so own the unborn?—Cool and casual through the hole in thin air closed at hotel room in London— Death reduces the college—Seriously considered so they are likely to face lung cancer disciplinary action—

Venus Vigar choked to death with part-time television —Ward boy kept his diary thoughts and they went back meticulously to the corridor—He pointed out that the whole world had already watched Identikit—"Why, we all take satisfaction—Rode a dancing horse on sugar avenue —Prettiest little thought you ever saw"—

The capsule was warm in Soho—An operation has failed to save American type jeans—Further talks today with practical cooperation—There are many similarities— Solicitor has ally at Portman Clinic—The Vital Clue that links the murders is JRR 284—Finished off in a special way just want to die—When his body was found three young men are still dancing the twist in The Swede's Dunedin muck spreading The New Zealand after 48 hours

in his bed sitter—Stephen film was in the hospital—
Definition of reasonable boy body between his denials—
Identity popped in flash bulb breakfast—Yards and yards
of entrails hung around the husband irrevocably committed
to the toilet—The Observer left his friend in Cocktail
Probation—Vanished with confessed folk singer—Studio
dresser John Vigar found dead on the old evacuation plan
—The body, used in 1939, year of Vigar's birth, was naked
—Both men had been neatly folded—As the series is soon
ending are these experiments really necessary? Uncontrolled flash bulbs popped in rumors—Said one: "All this
is typical Dolce just before Christ Vita—"—Quiet man in
624A said the tiny bedroom as doctor actor would never
do—Police examined the body counter outside little groups
of denials—Miss Taylor people hung around the husband
—He plays Mark even Anthony with Liz—There was great
bustle through the red hair—Born in Berlin and made his
first threat to peace at the age of 17—Hanratty was then
brought up as a Jew—Over 100 police in unfashionably
dressed women search for boy who had protested definition
of "reasonable friend" and "circumstantial police"—Prime
haggling going on—Sir, I am delighted to see that/writes
about/ I am quite prepared to/ Last attention is being
paid to routine foundations on the Square Generation/
The light woman is at the clear out/ if they wish to live
their moment without answering to me/ this of course
they will not do

James swaggering about in arson to be considered—
Murder in the operating theater at Nottingham—Stephen
said to be voting through yards and yards of entrails irrevocably committed to the toilet—

One More Chance?

Scientology means the study of "humanity's condition"
—Wise radio doctor—Logos Officers in his portable—The

Effects Boy's "scientology release" is locks over the Chinese—Told me to sit by Hubbard guide—

"What are you going to do?—That person going to get out of 'havingness??' "

Will cover the obvious usually sooner than later— Globe is self you understand until assumed unwittingly "reality" is made out of "Mr. Martin"—To agree to be Real *is* "real" and the way the flakes fall—Game conditions and no game every time—For him always been a game consists of "freed galaxies"—End getting an effect on the other team now ended—Look around here it's curtains for them—Be able to not know his past circumstances—Scio is knowing and wind hand to the hilt—Work we have logos you got it? Dia 'through noose —Jobbies would like to strike—Release certificate is issued for a respectable price—Find a process known as "overwhelming," what?—Come back work was what you could have—What would you permit that person—?? Food in The Homicide Act??—Look around and accept "one more chance?? "Havingness" bait and it's curtains —End anatomy of games—The fundamental reward business the bait—The cycle of "Humanity's condition"— Apparent because we believe it—One assumes a "beingness" over the Chinese—Like to strike a bargain: Other identities—Is false identity—In the end is just the same —Fundamentally agreement—All games for respectable share of these "barriers" and "purposes"—Know what they mean if they start "no-effect??"

Cool and casual the anatomy of games closed at hotel room in London—

The District Supervisor looked up with a narrow smile. "Sit down young man and smoke . . . occupational vice what? . . . only vice left us . . . You have studied Scientology of course?"

"Oh yes sir . . . It was part of our *basic* training sir . . . an unforgettable experience if you'll pardon the expression sir . . ."

147

"Repeat what you know about Scientology."

"The Scientologists believe sir that words recorded during a period of unconsciousness . . . (anesthesia, drunkenness, sleep, childhood amnesia for trauma) . . . *store* pain and that this pain store can be plugged in with key words represented as alternative mathematical formulae indicating number of exposures to the key words and reaction index, the whole battery feeding back from electronic computers . . . They call these words recorded during unconsciousness *engrams* sir . . . If I may say so sir the childhood amnesia for trauma is of special interest sir . . . The child *forgets* sir but since the controllers have the engram tapes sir any childhood trauma can be plugged in at any time . . . The pain that *overwhelms* that person is known as *basic basic* sir and when *basic basic* is wiped off the tape . . . Oh sir *then* that person becomes what they call a *clear* sir . . . Since Lord Lister sir . . . since the introduction of *anesthesia* sir . . ." (Amnesia smiled) "Oh let me yes sir tell you about a score of years' dust on the expression sir . . . If you'll pardon the expression sir are known as engrams sir."

"You have occupational experience?"

"Oh yes sir . . . It was part of our Basic Scientology Police Course sir"

"You have studied the risks of 'dancing'?"

"Sir the Scientologists believe this pain can be plugged in from Oaxaca photo copies and middle ages jacking off in deprostrated comrades"

(The living dead give a few cool hints . . . artificial arms and legs . . . soulless winded words)

"With the advent of *General Anesthesia* sir words recorded during *operations* became . . . (The nurse leans over the doctor's shoulder dropping cigarette ashes along the incision—'What are you looking for?' snarls the doctor . . . 'I know what I'm doing right enough . . . appendectomy at least . . . But why stop there?? Enemy anesthetized we advance . . . Fetch me another scalpel . . . This one's filthy . . .' Chorus of street boys outside: 'Fingaro?? one cigarette?? please thanks you very much . . . you like beeg one? . . . son bitch bastard . . .' 'Go away you villainous young toads' snarls the doctor pelting them with tonsils . . . 'Wish I had an uterine tumor . . . like a bag of cement . . . get one of them with any luck . . . You nurse . . . Put out that cigarette . . . *You wanta cook my patient's lungs out??"*

Shrill screams from maternity blast through the loud-speaker . . . The Technician mixes a bicarbonate of soda and belches into his hand . . . 'Urp urp urp . . . Fucking set picks up every fart and passes it along' A hideous sqwawk of death rattles smudges the instrument panel out of focus . . . White no smell of death from a cell of sick junkies in the prison wards swirls through the operating room . . . The doctor sags ominously severing the patient's femoral artery . . . 'I die . . . I faint . . . I fail . . . Fucking sick Coolies knock all the junk right out of a man . . .' He staggers towards the narco cabinet trailing his patient's blood . . . 'GOM for the love of God') It's a little skit I wrote for the *Post Gazette* sir . . . Anesthesia on stage sir words recorded during operations became the most reliable engrams . . . *Operation Pain* they called it sir . . . I can feel it now sir . . . in my tonsils sir . . . ether vertigo sir . . . (*The patient is hemorrhaging . . . nurse . . . the clamps . . . quick before I lose my patient*) . . . Another instrument of these pain tourists is the *signal switch* sir . . . what they call the 'yes no' sir . . . 'I love you I hate you' at supersonic alternating speed . . . Take orgasm noises sir and cut them in with torture and accident groans and screams sir and operating-room jokes sir and flicker sex and torture film right with it sir" . . .

"And what is your counter?"

"Just do it sir . . . in front of everybody sir . . . It

would have a comic effect sir . . . We flash a sex pic with torture in the background sir then snap that torture pic right in your bloody face sir . . . if you'll pardon the expression sir . . . we do the same with the sound track sir . . . *varying distances* sir . . . It has a third effect sir . . . right down the old middle line sir . . . if you'll pardon the expression sir . . . the razor inside sir . . .

"Jerk the handle . . . It sounds like this sir: 'Oh my God I can't stand it . . . That hurts that hurts that hurts so gooood . . . Oooooohhhh fuck me to death . . . Blow his fucking guts out . . . You're burning up baby . . . whole sky burning . . . I'll talk . . . Do it again . . . Come in . . . Get out . . . Slip your pants down . . . What's that?? *nurse* . . . the clamps . . . Cut it off . . . ' with the pics sir . . . popping like fireworks sir . . . sex and pain words sir . . . vary the tape sir . . . switch the tape sir . . .

Now all together *laugh laugh laugh* . . . Oh sir we *laugh* it right off the tape sir . . . We *forget* it right off the tape sir . . . You see sir we can *not know it* if we have the engram tapes sir . . . simple as a hiccup sir . . . melted a categorical no mercy for this enemy as dust and smoke sir . . . The man who never was reporting for no duty sir . . . A young cop drew the curtains sir . . . Room for one more operating-room joke inside sir"

You can still see the old operating room kinda run down now . . . Do you begin to see there is no patient there on the table?

Are These Experiments Necessary?

Saturday March 17, 1962, Present Time of Knowledge—Scio is knowing and open food in The Homicide Act—Logos you got it?—Dia through noose—England spent the weekend with a bargain before release certificate is issued—Dogs must be carried reluctant to the center—It's a grand feeling—There's a lot ended—This condition is best expressed queen walks serenely down dollar process known as overwhelming—What we want is Watney's Woodbines and the Garden Of Delights— And what could you have?—What would you? State of news?—Inquire on hospital? what?—Would you permit that person revived peat victory hopes of Fortria? Pre-clear to look around and discover Sheila's Cottage? —Death reduces the cycle of action—Venus Vigar choked to death in the direction of "havingness"—His diary thoughts they went back other identities—The whole world had valence is false identity—Further talks today with "barriers" and "purposes"—Vital clue that links the murders is: game one special way just want to die—Spreading the New Zealand after film was in the hospital—Yards of entrails hung about the toilet—The observer left his scio and vanished with confessed folk singer logos—Dia through noose found dead on the old evacuation—Release certificate of Vigar's birth is issued naked—This condition is best expressed uncontrolled flash bulbs popped process known as "overwhelming"—

"Sir I am quite prepared—other identities—Woman is at the clear out if is fundamentally agreement"—

"Look around here and tell me are these experiments really necessary?"—All this to "overwhelm"—? Apparency bustle through the red hair—I have said Scio Officers at any given time dictate place of years—Dead absolute need condition expressed process known as "overwhelming"—Silence—Don't answer—What could that person "overwhelm?"—Air?—The great wind revolving what you could have—What would you?—Sound and image flakes fall—It will be seen that "havingness" no more—

Paralyzed on this green land the "cycle of action"—
The cycle of last door—Shut off "Mr. Bradly Mr. Apparent Because We Believe It"—Into air—You are
yourself "Mr. Bradly Mr. Other Identities"—Action is
an apparency creating and aggravating conflict—Total
war of the past—I have said the "basic pre-clear identities" are now ended—Wind spirits melted "reality
need" dictates use of throat bones—"Real is real" do
get your heavy summons and are melted—Through all
the streets time for him be able to not know his past
walls and windows people and sky—Complete inten-
tions falling—Look around here—No more flesh scripts
dispense Mr.—Heard your summons—Melted "Mr.
Bradly Mr. Martin"

Melted into Air

Fade out muttering: "There's a lover on every corner
cross the wounded galaxies"—

Distant fingers get hung up on one—"Oh, what'll we
do?"

Slowly fading—I told him you on tracks—All over for
sure—I'm absolutely prophesized in a dream grabbing
Yuri by the shirt and throwing last words answer his
Yugoslavian knife—I pick up Shannon Yves Martin
may not refuse vision—Everybody's watching—But I
continue the diary—"Mr. Bradly Mr. Martin?"—You are
his eyes—I see suddenly Mr. Beiles Mr. Corso Mr. Burroughs presence on earth is all a joke—And I think:
"Funny—melted into air"—Lost flakes fall that were his
shadow: This book—No good junky identity fading out—

"Smoke is all, boy—Dont intersect—I think now I go
home and it's five times—Had enough slow metal fires—
Form has been inconstant—Last electrician to tap on the
bloody dream"—

"I see dark information from him on the floor—He pull out—Keep all Board Room Reports—Waiting chair to bash everybody—Couldn't reach tumescent daydream in Madrid—Flash a jester angel who stood there in 1910 straw words—Realize that this too is bad move—No good—No bueno—Young angel elevated among the subterraneans—Yes, he heard your summons—Nodded absently—"

"And I go home having lost—Yes, blind may not refuse vision to this book—"

Clom Fliday

I have said the basic techniques of nova are very simple consist in creating and aggravating conflicts— "No riots like injustice directed between enemies"—At any given time recorders fix nature of absolute need and dictate the use of total weapons—Like this: Collect and record violent Anti-Semitic statements—Now play back to Jews who are after Belsen—Record what they say and play it back to the Anti-Semites—Clip clap—You got it?—Want more? Record white supremacy statements—Play to Negroes—Play back answer—Now The Women and The Men—No riots like injustice directed between "enemies"—At any given time position of recorders fixes nature of absolute need —And dictates the use of total weapons—So leave the recorders running and get your heavy metal ass in a space ship—Did it—Nothing here now but the recordings—Shut the whole thing right off—*Silence*—When you answer the machine you provide it with more recordings to be played back to your "enemies" keep the whole nova machine running—The Chinese character for "enemy" means to be similar to or to answer—Don't answer the machine—Shut it off—

"The Subliminal Kid" took over the streets of the world —Cruise cars with revolving turrets telescope movie lenses and recorders sweeping up sound and image of the city around and around faster and faster cars racing through all the streets of image record, take, play back, project on walls and windows people and sky—And slow moving turrets on slow cars and wagons slower and slower record take, play back, project slow motion street scene—Now fast—Now slow—slower—*Stop*— Shut off—No More—My writing arm is paralyzed—No more junk scripts, no more word scripts, no more flesh scripts—He all went away—No good—No bueno— Couldn't reach flesh—No glot—Clom Fliday—Through invisible door—Adios Meester William, Mr. Bradly, Mr. Martin—

I have said the basic techniques creating and aggravating conflict officers—At any given time dictate total war of the past—Changed place of years in the end is just the same—I have said the basic techniques of Nova reports are now ended—Wind spirits melted between "enemies"—Dead absolute need dictates use of throat bones—On this green land recorders get your heavy summons and are melted—Nothing here now but the recordings may not refuse vision in setting forth—*Silence*—Don't answer—That hospital melted into air— The great wind revolving turrets towers palaces—Insubstantial sound and image flakes fall—Through all the streets time for him to forbear—Blest be he on walls and windows people and sky—On every part of your dust falling softly—falling in the dark mutinous "No more"—My writing arm is paralyzed on this green land—Dead Hand, no more flesh scripts—Last door— Shut off Mr. Bradly Mr.—He heard your summons— Melted into air—You are yourself "Mr. Bradly Mr. Martin—" all the living and the dead—You are yourself —There be—

Well that's about the closest way I know to tell you and papers rustling across city desks . . . fresh southerly winds a long time ago.

September 17, 1899 over New York

July 21, 1964
Tangier, Morocco

William Burroughs